ONLY THE CAT KNOWS

ONLY THE CAT KNOWS

Inspired by a true event in a single spring, 1970s, China

A NOVELLA

Ruyan Meng

Red Hen Press | *Pasadena, CA*

Book design and layout by Mark E. Cull

Library of Congress Cataloging-in-Publication Data

Names: Meng, Ruyan, author.
Title: Only the cat knows: inspired by a true event in a single spring, 1970s, China: a novella / Ruyan Meng.
Description: First edition. | Pasadena, CA: Red Hen Press, [2022]
Identifiers: LCCN 2022026222 (print) | LCCN 2022026223 (ebook) | ISBN 9781597098762 (paperback) | ISBN 9781597098779 (ebook)
Subjects: LCGFT: Novellas.
Classification: LCC PS3613.E485 O55 2022 (print) | LCC PS3613.E485 (ebook) | DDC 813/.6—dc23/eng/20220606
LC record available at https://lccn.loc.gov/2022026222
LC ebook record available at https://lccn.loc.gov/2022026223

The National Endowment for the Arts, the Los Angeles County Arts Commission, the Ahmanson Foundation, the Dwight Stuart Youth Fund, the Max Factor Family Foundation, the Pasadena Tournament of Roses Foundation, the Pasadena Arts & Culture Commission and the City of Pasadena Cultural Affairs Division, the City of Los Angeles Department of Cultural Affairs, the Audrey & Sydney Irmas Charitable Foundation, the Meta & George Rosenberg Foundation, the Albert and Elaine Borchard Foundation, the Adams Family Foundation, Amazon Literary Partnership, the Sam Francis Foundation, and the Mara W. Breech Foundation partially support Red Hen Press.

First Edition
Published by Red Hen Press
www.redhen.org

Human nature is not black and white, but black and grey.
—Graham Greene

ONLY THE CAT KNOWS

PROLOGUE

My father used to say that life was all about how you survive your *last straw*. I secretly disagreed. I never wanted to get to my last straw. (Well, who would?) But I never argued with him, either. There was no point in arguing with a rigid hard-ass.

When I was thirteen, he threw a teapot at my head. I endured fifteen stitches across my scalp because I'd dared to say a bad word in front of my mother. On another occasion, he forced me to kneel on the snow in my pajamas—I'd lied about something that I can no longer remember. I was saved by my sister then, as I flickered dreamily in and out of consciousness. She saw what was happening, and—with our mother—managed to manhandle me inside and tow me back to life.

To my father, I was a constant disappointment. I was never the son he thought he deserved.

The older I become the more I realize that life comes down to this: simplicity, enough food to eat, a roof over my head. I try to keep my life simple: it's how I've survived. I'd even forgotten all about my father's "last straw" notion, until . . .

ONE

He sat in the corner of the workshop, staring at the money in his hand: a few banknotes—varying in size—a few coins. Thirty-seven yuan and seventy-five cents. He counted it mechanically, several times. Thirty-seven yuan and seventy-five cents: no more, no less.

How many years had it been since the number had changed? Over a decade—a hundred and twenty-seven months, to be precise. The elliptical imprecision of thirty-seven and seventy-five had become a branded symbol in his mind, a numerical depiction of himself which—when recollected in the middle of the night—still retained the power to chill him from head to toe.

It was payday—that golden day with the smell of money in the air, mixed with a short-lived excitement, a temporary ease. He noticed his colleagues chatting in unusually good-humored tones: he spotted smiles lurking at the corners of some mouths, some faces. Break time was alive with chatter: even the workshop chief's habitual guard was down. Everyone seemed seduced by the sweet finny smell of money.

Accountant Liu, holding a thick stack of envelopes in his arms, stood at the doorway of the workshop calling out names and distributing envelopes. They fussed over him as if he were a celebrity—this sharp-witted, beaming fellow, a trustworthy Communist Party member. He was greatly liked by everyone, particularly on paydays.

Accountant Liu, who got a bonus this month? one man asked, opening his envelope, and avidly counting his takings.

Ask the chief, Liu said.

A strangled scream came from a woman who had counted her pay several times. When will you pay me? She questioned, eyes burning with anger. Again, again, my overtime wasn't paid!

I wasn't told to pay your overtime, Liu said, not glancing up.

But I should be paid, she retorted. I worked two Sundays!

Quit bothering me, Liu said, I have to concentrate. His voice sounded coarser, as if losing patience.

Give the chief's envelope to me, another man joked. I want a big fat one.

The big fat one's your wife, the workshop chief retorted, followed by a ribald burst of laughter.

From where he sat, he watched his colleagues, who mostly seemed to methodically mirror him: spittle on fingers, count, count, the thin dirty banknotes rustling between their fingers. Voices hissed around the workshop like gathering winds, nipping his ears, biting his skin.

Accountant Liu was about to leave when a woman cater-wauled: Master Liu, when will I get a raise? When?

Don't ask me, not my department, Liu said, and disappeared through the main door.

See you next month, sweet ass! The woman sniggered.

Truth was, he could not bring himself to ask the same question—and never so publicly—as that woman had. *Why have I never asked?* He leaned forward and the stool squeaked as he stretched his legs. His stool was worn and warped, its paint peeling; it could give way at any time. His legs started to shake fiercely as if from an internal convulsion. *I spend thousands of identical hours sitting on this damn thing, waiting for a simple number to change. It's payday, but nothing has changed.* Something salty and sour curdled his throat, he spat.

His secret mantra was always "next month." *Next month it will surely happen. Next month I swear I'll do something about it.* Yet next month never arrived. He seemed frozen in time, a mere number, while life aged around him.

Sunlight fell greasily through a row of high windows, smudging over the dusty brick walls and looming shadows of the machines. He had noticed a hole on one of the windowpanes a few days before, which had multiplied and stretched out like spider legs. He'd seen omens before in cracked glass.

From across the corridor, several female coworkers had gathered, teasing and clamoring. The workshop chief had cracked a joke, presumably a daring one. The crowd responded with boos, hisses, laughter. A shriveled woman tweaked his ear with a grin, then squeezed his waist. Despite her age, she had a pleasant voice. He also enjoyed talking to her—simply to hear the resonance in her voice.

He returned the money and pay slip to the envelope and stuck it inside his jacket pocket. It felt as if the numbers themselves were pressing into him. He felt weighted, perhaps with dread, or as if he was running out of something—time, perhaps.

Shaking the stiffness from his legs, he wandered restlessly throughout the workshop, his senses abnormally acute, a wildcat roused by the scent of flesh. There was still that patch of machine oil saturating the concrete floor. The oily stain had been trapped between two tool racks and had, over time, become covered with a thick layer of dust, which formed an irregular, almost furry shape, like peeled skin from some dead animal—as if a giant rat had made a wild dart into a hole, leaving part of its skin behind. Nausea swept over him at the thought of rats, twisting, agile, surging beneath the floor.

More raucous laughter from the crowds in the distance. Lifting his eyes, he saw that shriveled woman's hand caressing the chief's back, her hands caked with black machine oil. He couldn't help glancing down at his own hands, which were similarly encrusted. The stench of oil suddenly seemed everywhere.

There was a half-smoked cigarette at the foot of the tool

rack—Xiao Yang had probably thrown it down. He cursed at the lack of respect, looked about, then retrieved it. Striking a match to light the cigarette stub seemed to fire the same four numbers in his head, four numbers, with a long squirrel-like tail: thirty-seven and seventy-five.

His pay slip comprised of a narrow piece of peat-brown paper, perhaps two feet long and a half-inch wide. The typographic font resembled a muddle of ants: his basic wage, his extra wage, his labor protection subsidy, his heating allowance, his cooling allowance, his overtime wage, his special skill wage, his travel allowance, his Labor Union dues, his Communist Party membership dues, his Communist Youth League membership dues, his holiday wage, his child care fees, his dormitory fees, his sick leave deduction, his absenteeism deduction—all the socialist bureaucratic nonsense that he had cursed a thousand times in his head.

None of these figures mattered beyond the final three: a basic wage of thirty-eight yuan, the Labor Union's twenty-five cents due automatically deducted, leaving thirty-seven yuan and seventy-five cents. These digits, yoked as Siamese twins, never altered; their contours never changed.

He was classified, as was almost everyone else in the factory, as working-class—a true member of the proletariat. It was therefore his duty to pay the Labor Union fee each month. He often thought that the combined dues must provide a pretty reasonable income for the Labor Union. Yet what they did with the dues collected, year after year, remained a mystery.

Baba, your pay slip looks like a piece of hair, brown hair, his younger daughter once teased him, dancing with it in her hand.

A child's imagination was incredible: he could not understand how a piece of brown paper could resemble hair. Yet, after that, the little girl gleefully saved his pay slips and made pigtails out of them, binding them nimbly together with a rubber band. She wore the paper pigtail atop her own braids and ran around the room, giggling.

Lulu's pigtails have more hair than mine, she whispered one day. He knew exactly what she meant even before she added, Lulu collects two pay slips a month.

Lulu was his sister's daughter, and his younger daughter's playmate. They accumulated their parents' pay slips diligently, making pigtails, which sometimes appeared on their dolls' heads, instead of their own.

Your mother doesn't have a pay slip! Your mother doesn't have a job! Lulu screeched one day, while the girls were playing. Bewildered, he thought, *How could she say such a cruel thing?* Everyone in the room froze, and Lulu—appalled—fled.

It was true, of course. Perhaps this was the reason why the payday pigtails never got mixed-up.

It's obvious that the girls knew just how much their parents made, yelling the figures out—comparing the figures, for sure. But the difference in salary was unsurprising, because his sister and her husband were college graduates, members of the Communist Party, and worked for government departments. His brother-in-law, who often traveled for his job, also received travel allowances—he was probably earning twice his own salary.

One day, his younger daughter, sporting both Lulu's pigtail and her own, stood in front of the mirror, swaying from side to side while humming a revolutionary song.

Lulu's pigtail looks much better than yours, his elder daughter said viciously, as if in revenge for something.

Sometimes that girl is absolutely cruel, he thought, flushing with shame. Hastily, he lit a cigarette, as he never wished to show his emotion in front of his children. His younger daughter ignored her sister: pigtails still atop her head, she stood before the mirror—shaking, jiggling, singing. When he caught sight of her in the mirror it was as if the pigtails were two shaggy monsters, grinning mockingly at him.

Every month payday approached him like a phantom, enveloping him into a fog of nervous abstraction and turning him into an amnesiac. He forgot that he'd left the power on while fixing the light switch in Aunt Li's. He took his younger daughter to the doctor, paid for her prescription but left the medicine on the counter. One morning he arrived at work empty-handed, having left his bag and lunchbox at home. He parked his bicycle outside the shops without even locking it. In the workshop, he spent some time probing fruitlessly around for the caliper until Xiao Yang reminded him, with a curious little laugh, that it was on his bench behind him. At these times he felt both irritated and vaguely ridiculous.

Late one evening, after three nights of insomnia, he asked for sleeping pills at a drugstore.

For yourself? the pretty woman asked, from behind the counter. The store was otherwise empty, though a clerk sat behind the cashier desk in the corner, nodding off over his newspaper.

Yes, he said. The resonance of medicinal herbs—or his lack of sleep—made his head spin.

One per day for a week, she said, her lips curving blithely. He looked at her while she put white pills from a glass jar into a small paper bag. Her hands were wrinkle-free and well-manicured—a pair of bourgeois hands, the kind any man would wish to touch.

Only seven?

That's all I can give you.

Are they really so strong? he said, pretending casualness.

Yes, this shit is dan-ger-ous, she drawled in an amusing way and then blushed, as if to apologize for her coarseness. He gazed back, thinking, *She's lovely.*

How many does it take? He asked, attempting to detain her longer.

For what?

You know what I mean.

Uh, oh!—her mouth remained half-open as she suddenly realized. She hesitated, then: Ten, maybe fifteen? Why do you want to know?

I'm—inquisitive. He charmed her with a smile and left.

He took two of the pills before bed but still woke up in the middle of the night, aware of the pale shadows and icy silhouettes filtering through the thin, moonlit curtains. He tossed and turned, his bedclothes itching. He felt as if he was falling into a strange half-world, where all consciousness of himself as an individual was lost. No, he was no longer real—he was just another cog in the factory machine—he was only the sum of two numbers, thirty-seven and seventy-five.

He argued with himself:

Who struck terror into your heart, fool?

I'm not in terror—I'm in hopes—next month is coming!

What could a man as pusillanimous as you hope for? Next month or any month?

I don't know. It's a dream, I admit.

How could any fool—sitting on the same stool for ten years—dream dreams for so many years and still dare to call it hope?

He shifted to the edge of the bed, probing the paper bag for more pills, thinking *I may not need these after the next payday.* This was the time period when hope erupted, the fabled "next month"—at least briefly—sparking a fire across his brain, which later evaporated, like a coil of smoke from a cigarette.

Half-closing his eyes, he recalled the girl's lovely face and soft bourgeois hands. Gradually, long dormant desire flared through him. He slid his hands under the quilt and started to gently caress his wife, who slept between him and their son. To his surprise, she was more alert than he expected: she squirmed and nervously pushed his hands away. What are you doing? she murmured, shifting away from him toward their son.

He drew back, feeling as chilled as her skin. There was no warmth between them. The months of thwarted hopes and long waiting had dissipated the longing that they had once had for each other. He thought, *Even a hedgehog might have sources of happiness that I lack.*

He turned and gazed again at the iced moon through the curtains.

I'll go back to her for more pills, next week.

TWO

He carried his nightmares with him to work. He had bad dreams even when napping in the workshop during lunch hour. In one, he stumbled on the gravel, rammed his head against a wall and bled—with relief instead of pain. In another he was pulled by a malevolent force into a chill, green-frothed river, descending effortlessly; in a third he stood quivering on the brink of a pit, watching his body being slowly sucked into a whirlpool of indefiniteness.

In his dreams he also saw his father—youthfully taut, stern-faced—who offered him a cigarette without a word. When he could bear the silence no longer, he started talking: surprisingly enough, his father listened.

It's not that I never dreamed. I did. I used to dream I had gone south—to a place near the sea, to live in the sun. You know I've always wanted a family. And I have a family now, but, but . . . he stopped, shaken by the undisguised contempt in his father's eyes. He shuddered to wakefulness with a groan, longing to be once again kneeling in the snow, experiencing again that blissful suspension of consciousness.

As his broken nights and distracted days mounted up, he sometimes became obsessed by niggling worries: *What would I do if my bicycle had a flat tire? It costs two cents to pump it up, which I don't have. How can I not even have two cents? I'd just have to stand at the side of the road and lie: Excuse me, I'm so sorry, but I've got a flat tire, and I left my wallet at home. Would you mind letting me . . . haha . . . hahaha!*

And he'd fake an ironic little laugh, then giggling at himself. He practiced playing at his life, a failed actor—only afterward becoming morose. *Surely I'm simply denying my levels of self-neglect. How long can this crazy charade go on?*

He took a perverse pleasure in rehearsing his role, altering his voice, warping his mouth and mumbling under his breath. *I'll be ready to be a beggar when the time comes*, he told himself, with a strange lightheartedness.

He felt most on edge during the penniless days toward the end of each month. He salvaged his cigarette ends, which he stored in a brown envelope, rolling the wispy dregs inside the rags of an old calendar when he had no money left at all. When the lunch bell rang, he contrived to be the last to leave the workshop, so that he could retrieve the cigarette stubs littering the floor without being observed. Despite his care, however, he was caught by Xiao Yang one day. As he bent down to pocket one, Xiao Yang waltzed in quietly from the toilet.

Oh! Oh, I—I forgot my—my meal ticket! Xiao Yang stuttered and rushed on.

He felt enraged at Xiao Yang, half convincing himself that his apprentice was spying on him, cursing his bad luck. *Little prick. I should have never taken him in as my apprentice in the first place!* Briefly, he felt an unreasonable urge to lash out at someone as he sat on his stool, without appetite for lunch. Sometimes it seemed to him that he was nothing more than a starving stray dog, sniffing for money everywhere.

Of course, he could ask his wife for money from time to time, but he was reluctant, as he knew that she always had very little extra in hand. Sometimes she had to borrow money from the neighbors, just to put food on the table.

After Xiao Yang's intrusion on his cigarette salvaging, he was intrigued to find himself counting banknotes in his head, as though playing some childish game. He imagined the various notes (not many) that he would get on payday—three ten-yuan, one five-yuan, two one-yuan and seventy-five cents, or seven five-yuan, two one-yuan and seventy-five cents. The combination of thirty-seven and seventy-five was thaumaturgic to him. He imagined how he would finger every banknote that he might be gifted with, whisking them about like magic playing cards. In his mind, he laid them in neat little rows and columns—then shuffled and started all over again. He preferred new notes over old ones, suspecting that the crackle of new notes might give him more pleasure, even some sort of luck. How he relished the anticipation of counting, the fresh spittle damp on his fingers! At other times, however, thirty-seven and seventy-five could no longer entrance him. Then the numbers remained as heavy as destiny, pressing down on him, a boulder on his chest. Ten years of it—ten long years!

His imagined pay raise possessed him, day and night. He grinned to himself whenever he thought of forty-seven, fifty-seven—even sixty-seven! And yet, a mere ten yuan a month more would make a big difference. His wife could use ten yuan to buy eggs, milk, meat, and sugar—foods with all the nutrition that his children needed.

Every now and then his wife would let slip that one of their neighbors, so-and-so, had been promoted, or had become a member of the Communist Party, or had received a raise. Whenever that happened, her face was burnished with what appeared to be almost ecstatic envy—half-desire, half-reproach—an oblique reflection of his own despondence. He was offended by the scorn she could barely conceal—and secretly convinced that she only shared such gossip out of spite.

Despite the insipid smile plastered on her face, her eyes still seemed to challenge him, sneering: *When will* you *get a raise?* At such times he was at a loss for words, undermined, almost demolished, by the latent fire in those eyes. Was she secretly furious at him? If so, why did her eyes speak and her lips say nothing?

At times like these, he seemed to feel surrounded by invisible wires of anxiety from which he could no longer extricate himself.

Early one morning, he felt uneasy for no discernible reason. His stomach ached; his cigarette tasted nauseating. At breakfast, his wife directed a steely, unreadable smile toward him. *What did that smile mean?* he puzzled. *Ah, it's her hint about payday. I get it.*

He left for work, leaving his lunch box on the dining table.

The north wind shivered him as he weaved among the morning crowds. He couldn't help picturing in his mind how the city would look when winter—that season of obstinate coldness and unremitting desolation—eventually came: the lifeless sun cloaking the sky, the half-melted snow transitioning into blackened ice-sludge on the road, the dust, soot and trash papers skidding on the wind, the shops emitting a miasma of warm filth and stale coal into the air, and gray-shadowed men and women (he—undeniably—one of them) spitting out the fetid mucus clogging their throats. His wife's smile itself had seemed wintry, foreshadowing the long, harsh winter to come.

He loathed winter—as did his eldest daughter—because they could never afford enough coal to keep the family warm. Once winter came, all five spent long weary nights together, huddled in a single room. There were days when he wished he could hibernate through winter, covering his body with leaves and mud, enduring the winter by himself until it eased, like a long illness.

As winter crept closer, his elder daughter became increasingly cranky and taciturn, showing open hostility, almost hatred, toward everyone. She hung an old sheet to screen her side of the twin bed that she shared with her sister. After dinner she immediately burrowed under the covers, moaning to herself. Later she would pick a fight with her sister, yelling: Move your stupid leg away from me! or Back off, brat, you take up too much space! Tension and affliction floated like motes in the air. He seemed to sense his daughter's eyes, moist with resentment and contempt, staring at him through her thin sheet.

They all grew increasingly silent in winter, as if their tongues had been immobilized, by cold or by distress. Except for a few dramatic screams from his elder daughter—Not so close! You're always too close! Did you just fart? You stink-bug!—their home endured a chilled, almost unbearable, quiet.

Sometimes, at the end of an endless winter evening, he would go to his shack, standing as if mesmerized before a stack of frosted cabbage, smoking and feeling himself. A thin twist of white mist swirled around him as he breathed shallowly, half-panting, trying to relocate the sense of his own existence that had long since disappeared when among his family.

He no longer hurried home after work, missing supper. He loafed around aimlessly on his bike, cold, withdrawn and hungry. Sometimes he took the roads in the opposite direction, passing through streets he had known since his childhood. One evening he stopped by his former high school, now a community hospital. He dismounted and slouched against the wall, watching people passing by. He could hear his voice as a youth: unmoored, jaunty, remote. *My future is somewhere in the south—dazzling sunlight, a warm city, the sea.*

It was what he had told his father, who had never listened. His hands stroked the blackened, wrecked bricked wall of his old school. It still felt familiar to his hands, though patched with cold concrete after twenty years of vicissitudes.

If only I'd gone to college from this place, if only I graduated as an engineer, if only I was living in some city in the south . . . So many meaningless if-onlys! *Shit, I'm not living my life only to prove that my father is right!* He spat in the air[1] three times, in hopes of changing his luck—or possibly to lose his sense of being ill-omened. Yet, all the way home, if-only questions still teased his brain.

The previous evening he'd taken a wrong turn going home and cycled at least two miles before noticing. He had ended up in a completely strange neighborhood: a narrow street crisscrossing a messy construction site, alongside dilapidated

---

1 Spit in the air: a Chinese way to say "knock on wood."

mud-roofed houses and narrow alleyways, children playing in the dust by the side of the street.

He got off the bicycle, suddenly confused, and for a long, mad moment considered walking with his back facing the road ahead (which ended in a construction dump), his eyes searching the shadows behind him. Disturbed, he felt dogged by some latent adversity—something menacing and unknown—something intent upon making even Workers Village[2] distant, unreachable.

He turned into a wider street where dim streetlights had just come on. Parking his bicycle by a lamppost, he withdrew into shadow, his back against a wall. The night air was filled with breezy dust. He looked into the sky, where the stars speckled, and seemed to retreat into the distance, a quiet death. There was music playing from somewhere: a few workers hurried past. He took some old calendar paper and a little fag-end tobacco from his pocket and rolled a cigarette. After a single pull, he was suddenly in a buoyant mood. *Maybe I'll buy a pack of new cigarettes tomorrow, after I'm paid. Maybe I'll get a raise this month.*

He heard muffled footsteps coming from an alleyway. A thin boy, aged perhaps ten or twelve, wearing an oversized ragged winter coat, glanced at him alertly, and then stopped.

---

2   Worker Villages were barrack-like, modular, house units built in Communist China from the 1950s to 1980s, based on an architectural concept copied from the Soviet Union.

Hello, the boy said.

He looked at the boy but didn't say anything.

Can I have that? The boy asked, pointing at the cigarette. He had a strong southern accent and pale lips formed into a pleading smile.

He raised his hand. You mean this? You want to smoke?

Yes.

You're just a kid.

No, I'm not a kid. Just give it to me please, the boy said, eyes fixed on him strangely.

He hesitated for a second, then: Here, take it.

The boy grabbed it and sucked immediately, the white smoke swift out of his nostrils. He moved closer, squatting down against the wall.

You aren't local, are you? he asked.

I was hungry, the boy murmured. Now I feel better.

The cigarette had torched almost to the end, but he still held it with the tips of his thumb and forefinger.

How old are you? Twelve, thirteen?

I'm sixteen, the boy said firmly, dropping the cigarette end to the ground. What does it matter?

Where are you from?

The south.

Where in the south?

What's the difference? South is south.

Do you have family here?

What do you think, the boy said in disgust.

Just asking.

They remained in companionable silence. On impulse he rolled another cigarette and handed it to the boy. Cigarettes can cure hunger, he said, believe me.

Still, it's not food, the boy said, sticking the cigarette on his ear.

How did you end up in this city?

I don't remember.

I wanted to live in the south when I was your age, he said vaguely. Bright sunshine, trees, flowers all year long, warm—not freezing cold in winter like we have here.

You're crazy, the boy mocked. You know nothing! Winter in the south is ten times worse—there, the dank coldness can freeze your balls. We never have stoves: we all get chilblains. And when it starts to rain, it never stops—it rains for months and months! It's not until the sun comes out that you realize you're still alive.

Stunned, his eyes shifted to study the derisive expression on the boy's childlike face, while his mind drifted to the past.

My brother-in-law was always travelling to the south, and he doesn't agree, he said, in defense of his old dream.

What is he then?—not that it matters. I'm still hungry. Do you have one or two cents?

He looked at the boy, whose smile seemed sincere, yet his

eyes had sharpened, with the distasteful cunning of a home-less drifter.

I don't have a cent.

You don't even have one cent? The boy was annoyed.

What could you do with one cent, anyway?

One cent can do a lot of things, the boy said. At least I could buy a piece of candy, maybe two.

He stood up and brushed down his jacket.

Hey, don't go. I never wanted free money from you, the boy wheedled, taking a little harmonica from his coat pocket. Here, sit down. I'll play a song if you give me two cents. I'm a good player.

He said nothing and moved toward his bicycle.

Come back, the boy yelled, almost desperately. All right, then, one cent! I'll play you a revolutionary song for one cent. The boy followed him to the lamppost.

I told you that I have no money, he said, pulling his bicycle off the curb. To be honest with you, I'm hungry myself.

Do you have any food at all, anything that I could eat?

No, I have nothing, he said, slapping his pocket.

Let me have your match, at least, the boy said, giving him a malign look.

He took out his matchbox and held it out.

The boy grabbed it and stepped back into the shadows. As he rode away, he heard the soft, plangent sound of a har-monica wailing on the breeze. It was certainly no revolution-

ary song and the loneliness in the music pierced him like a
long-forgotten wound.

THREE

He tensed, fingers suddenly tapping edgily on his lap as he watched Lao Qi stride toward his bench. An alleged Rightist during the Anti-Rightist Campaign—despite having been detained in hard labor camps for six years—Lao Qi was perpetually jovial, his big teeth and dry, thick lips making his smile even more noticeable. He wore the dirtiest and smelliest uniform in the factory—a buttonless jacket, his pants tied with hemp, along with a pair of laceless rubber shoes with holes at their heels. His was an unmistakable tread, scuffing along in those ancient shoes.

Professor, you need a woman to clean you up, coworkers had used to joke, before his marriage.

Lao Qi would say obstinately: I'm clean already!

He had recently married a pretty widow with two young children, who was already pregnant. Yet since his marriage, nothing had changed. He wasn't like some intellectuals—there was no flaunting of books, no elaborate charade of knowledge—instead there was something truthful and unworldly in that beaming gaze.

As the head of Fraternity[3], he voluntarily collected the dues and distributed the lump sum collected, keeping records in his meticulous handwriting, and rarely making a single mistake.

Hello, Mr. Right! (Mr. Right was his nickname, as a Rightist).

Hello, time for the dues, Lao Qi said, waving a small pouch which had started life as flour sacking. Five yuan. Fraternity dues . . . Are you all right? You look tired.

I'm fine, he said, handing him a five yuan note. How's Mrs. Right?

She's well. How about your kids? Lao Qi opened the pouch, inserted the money and made two neat ticks in his notebook.

They're better, he said. His son had suffered acute nephritis the previous fall—and then, within a month, his younger daughter had been diagnosed with pleurisy.

Don't you worry, Lao Qi advised. They'll recover quickly, trust me. Kids are vigorous creatures.

They are.

Try one of these! Lao Qi said, taking out an expensive cigarette pack and offering it to him.

Oh, good stuff.

Just at that moment, though, he felt a little dizzy, so he

---

3   The Fraternity was a private, self-organized fellowship intended to enable mutual financial aid. Each member paid monthly dues, with the lump sum collected awarded to each member in turn. Those enduring illness, hardship or family emergency took precedence.

stuck it behind his ear, suddenly recollecting the young beggar he'd met near the construction site.

From the chairman of the Labor Union, Lao Qi said, smiling. I helped him write a speech for the Party conference, and he sent me two packs! Two! Eh, you don't happen to know where I could buy some eggs? My wife needs some extra nutrition, and they're out of stock at our grocers.

He paused for a second and then said: Well, you know the City Hall, right?

Yes.

You pass that building and go on eastward for six blocks, turn left at the Post Office, and about five hundred meters until you spot a small alley with a drug store just before it. Take a sharp right into that alley, then keep going until you pass a small park. At the western corner of the park, there's a burned-down church. Every Thursday after dark, as long as there's no rain, there's a black market there. Try your luck next Thursday. You might be lucky.

All right, I will!

Can you remember how to get there?

I surely do, Lao Qi smiled. Thanks!—I appreciate it.

One egg per day costs about five yuan a month, he said suddenly.

Every evening he watched his wife cutting a boiled egg in half. His son and younger daughter would sit by the table, relishing their egg slowly and dreamily while his elder daughter stood a distance, chewing her bottom lip with a venomous look in her beautiful eyes.

Yes, a little expensive, isn't it, said Lao Qi.

You're telling me, he said, recollecting the six yuan he spent on milk every month. The drama and indignation caused by the milk was still more disruptive to family life. With a special hospital coupon, his wife was allowed to daily order an eight-ounce bottle of milk for their sick son and younger daughter to share. He'd even seen neighbors nudging each other and staring enviously at the empty milk bottles on their windowsill.

I'd rather be sick and get my share of milk, his elder daughter had blurted at the dinner table one evening, shocking everyone. Smirking, she'd seemed to be taking vindictive pleasure in riling everyone in the room.

Well, you're welcome to my share, his younger daughter had snapped, her face flushing. I'd rather go to school and be allowed to play outside!

Your share of what? Your share of pleurisy, or your share of milk? His elder daughter had mocked, near-hatred in her eyes.

Both! You can have both!

Stop it, their mother had ordered. Stop being so nasty to your sister!

He'd suddenly stopped chewing, pushed back his chair

and walked outside, lighting a cigarette as he went. His wife had watched him leave, too shocked to say anything . . .

So, what are you busy with now? Lao Qi asked, crushing his cigarette end underfoot, one of his bare toes emerging from his disreputable shoes.

Oh, little things here and there, he said. Always something, you know.

He looked away from Lao Qi's feet. *Surely his wife could repair those shoes for him or get him to wear a pair of socks? Marriage normally makes a man look better cared-for, not worse!*

Lao Qi said, Well, I hate to bother you, but if you have a little spare time, I wonder if you could carpenter a small window for me.

What for?

My wife cooks in the open air. It's very difficult when it rains. I'd like to build a shack for her to use as a kitchen. Lao Qi grinned.

He found this constant merriment baffling. *Was the fellow never worried about anything?*

I can do it. Just find the wood and the glass and let me know. Then he added swiftly: So, what are you doing with the Fraternity money?

He hadn't intended this: the words seemed to fly from his mouth, as unruly as children. He was shocked, even disgusted, but it wasn't the first time this had happened. He had recently felt compelled to ask others about private matters—in particular, about how they spent their money.

Lao Qi only chuckled.

A sewing machine—that's the plan! I've been saving for years, and I promised her a sewing machine before we got married. Now she's nagging me about it—but I'm on the waiting list for a ration stamp. Women, eh? They're so demanding! I just don't know how to deal with them!

The sewing machine is a good idea, he said. You should buy her one.

He attempted to chuckle too, though his voice no longer seemed under his control. It was as if some other voice was stealthily inserting itself into his larynx. Also, he couldn't help thinking, *My wife also wants a sewing machine.* The cost?—he didn't even dare to think about it.

Did you buy anything special with yours? Lao Qi asked.

Not really, he admitted. His wife had spent most of their Fraternity money before the last Spring Festival—it was long since gone. They had bought no bicycles, sewing machines or other luxury goods; instead, they'd spent every penny on nutritious food and medicine for their son and daughter.

Has your wife found any work yet?

Not yet, though she's begging everyone to spread the word. She's tried really hard.

The truth was, his wife used to babysit for neighbors, making twenty to thirty yuan a month. But since the children's illnesses no one had asked her, perhaps secretly fearing that acute nephritis—or else pleurisy—might be contagious. It had been seven months since she had worked. At first, she had merely wept around the home, but later frustration had set in, and she had rushed about Worker Village, emphatically denying that either of the children's illnesses was infectious.

Women are more resilient than we know, Lao Qi told him.

Yes, and more realistic too, he said.

His wife had constantly reiterated what she'd heard about this malnutrition business, ever since the children had fallen sick. Her arguments were perfectly familiar to him, so familiar that it surprised him that they could still wound him so deeply.

The doctors say that the kids suffer from malnutrition, she said, over and over. Their immune systems are weak—that's why they got so sick in the first place! Also, they're both underweight and shorter than most. A sorrowful sigh usually followed these remarks, which made his skin tingle. Yet it was not he alone whom she was blaming. He was conscious of the guilt and self-reproach in her tone, as if it was *her* fault that their children were suffering. The guilt—if not the pleurisy—was certainly contagious enough!

Our kids are suffering from malnutrition, she repeated, in moods of resignation, fury or deep despair—as though determined to keep his own illness permanently inflamed. *Mal-*

nutrition, malnutrition, malnutrition! he shouted back, but only deep inside. In fact, he never scolded his wife, and they hardly ever quarreled; instead, they burned.

Lao Qi said, hey, if you ever need anything, just let me know.

Sure, he said.

He used to borrow money from Lao Qi when he was short of cash, but he hadn't done so since his marriage. He thought, *A married man is another version of man.* And he coughed, resting his hand on his chest as if to touch a deeper pain.

Meanwhile his apprentice, Xiao Yang, returned from the toilet. He generally went to the toilet six or seven times a day, remaining there as long as he dared, as if yearning to remain indefinitely. Xiao Yang had confided that he had been born with a gastrointestinal problem which meant that he couldn't hold anything in his stomach for long . . . but he suspected that the toilet was nothing more than an excuse for the youngster's laziness.

Hi, professor, Xiao Yang said, patting Lao Qi on the shoulder. You're busier than Accountant Liu on payday.

Nothing like, Lao Qi said. He works for the Party; I do this for fun.

If they hold a referendum on model workers in our factory, professor, you'd get far more votes than Liu.

He agreed: For sure. Bet on it.

Lao Qi mocked them: How can I be a model worker? I was in camp for six years.

Don't tell me that, Xiao Yang said. Who wouldn't have been? Look at Liu: his certificates and awards cover his office's walls—he gets a raise more often than any of us, not to mention all those bonuses. He got a three-bedroom flat last month—three big bedrooms, a private kitchen, and a toilet. How good is that?

You have to be a Party member first, Lao Qi reminded him. And a model worker.

A model worker goes to the toilet only once a day, he mocked his apprentice. Xiao Yang's face turned very pink, but he said nothing.

Five yuan, comrade, said Lao Qi, waving his pouch at Xiao Yang.

Professor, you are the world's worst debt collector, Xiao Yang half-joked, searching for money in his pockets.

Ha ha. So what are you going to buy with your Fraternity money? Lao Qi asked Xiao Yang, as he counted up his dues.

He wants to buy a bicycle, he rushed in, answering for Xiao Yang. *It's that stupid voice again*, he thought, exasperated. Sewing machines . . . bicycles . . . bicycles . . . sewing machines. The brutal senselessness of words flipped through his head as Xiao Yang confirmed it with a smirk.

Yes, it's true. I have to buy a bicycle this year. As it is, I get cramped on crowded buses with a whole bunch of annoying mares who squeeze my butt off every day. I'm getting sick and tired of it, I can tell you.

You? You're as thin as a chick. What butt are you talking about? Lao Qi laughed, slapping Xiao Yang on the buttock. All three chortled.

Take this morning, Xiao Yang said, becoming more animated: Just this morning I gave up my seat to this bitch with a baby. She didn't even bother to thank me! Shit, you can't even imagine how rank she smelled, like baby poop marinated in sour milk. As soon as she sat down, she started breastfeeding. Some chicks behind me pushed so hard I had to flatten myself against her!

So, what'd she do? he said, genuinely curious. Did she slap you?

No, but she flipped out and cursed me. It's what I have to put up with every day.

What did you do after that? Lao Qi asked.

What did I do? Nothing. What *could* I do? I just gave a dirty look to her big meaty boob.

You rutting rascal. Lao Qi grinned. They laughed, Xiao Yang loudest of all.

Xiao Yang was the third apprentice he'd trained in the past decade. He was a recognized master worker in the workshop: skilled, knowledgeable, and excellent at his work. Taking on apprentices gave him a sense of dignity, and he was comforted by the certainty that he was paid much more than they. However, at the end of their three-year apprenticeship, when his apprentices were, overnight, transformed into not only a colleague but into a colleague earning precisely the same wage as he was, he felt ashamed, even mortified. Each time this happened, his sense of being a master worker was shaken. Perhaps for this reason, he intentionally kept a certain distance between himself and his former apprentices. Secretly, he even blamed the apprentices—not only his own, but every one of them—for robbing him of his raise. *They are no longer your apprentices, but competitors and snitches instead. Nothing's worse than that!*

When his first apprentice married, he'd been invited to the wedding. Unwilling as he'd been to go, such an invitation had been impossible to refuse, and he'd reluctantly attended. At the wedding dinner, he'd acted like an utter fool, becoming tipsier and tipsier—eventually engaging in a furious row with a fellow guest, for no good reason, a man almost as drunk as he. By the time his colleagues had finally sent him home, he'd been almost unconscious. The next morning, stricken with remorse and feeling degraded in the eyes of the newlyweds and his colleagues, he had decided that he owed everyone an abject apology. However, he'd kept his head down for a few days, hesitating and debating with himself, before finally deciding to let the matter rest. He strode about the workshop with a straight back and impassive face, feeling covertly watched from every direction, thinking *I've no intention of apologizing for what I've done—whether right or wrong.*

That's all. To his intense relief, no one ever mentioned his embarrassing behavior—not in his presence, at least.

The son of the workshop's director had himself married a few months previously; and the workers had agreed on a whip-round of one yuan each to purchase a wedding gift. Unluckily, Lao Qi came to collect his share on one of his penniless days.

I left my wallet at home, he'd said, with a feigned smile, thinking ironically: *the excuse I composed and rehearsed has finally been put to good use!*

Xiao Yang had generously paid his share, as well as his own. He swore he'd pay him back the next day. But, the business dragged on until the next payday. During those two weeks, whenever he'd been obliged to speak to Xiao Yang, he'd always lowered his head, refusing to meet his eyes. He'd also avoided him as much as possible, while at the same time attempting to pretend that nothing had happened.

During those weeks, Xiao Yang had often appeared to deliberately confront him, a perverse grin on his face. Gradually, Xiao Yang's high voice and tittering laugh—even his exaggerated facial expressions—had become unbearable. He'd not been able to move for imagining that Xiao Yang's mocking gaze was following him, that his crooked eyebrow was lifted in his direction.

I'm out of cash to buy a meal ticket, Xiao Yang had yelled half-jokingly, half-sarcastically, one day during break. When he'd stood up from his bench, briefly stretched, and gone to the toilet, he'd felt Xiao Yang's sardonic gaze fixated on his retreating back.

A swarm of flies had hummed around him as he squatted in his stall. He'd thought, *Even the red-eyed flies seem to recognize me as some shameless and meaningless creature, not fully human.* He'd crushed the newspaper in his hands until his fingers were riddled with black ink, and wiped his butt so spitefully that it had ached for the rest of the day.

Since this episode it seemed that something had marked him. A single glance at Xiao Yang's face, a glimpse of a newspaper, or even a fly, would trigger nausea, a near-despair, related either to his debt or to his vanishing hope for next month's raise.

The giggling of his younger daughter and her cousin Lulu—they were again making pigtails with pay slips—utterly infuriated him. It was also hard to resist the impulse to lash out at his elder daughter upon observing her goading her sister.

At work, he kept Xiao Yang busy with simple and monotonous work, keeping his actual training to the absolute minimum, while his reticence seemed to foster a sense of unease. As soon as the lunch bell rang, he left off whatever he was doing and walked off without a word to the canteen, leaving Xiao Yang looking after him in almost pathetic bewilderment.

In the bathhouse, he stepped in the shower, touching his bony flesh with rough hands and feeling like weeping. *I'm no longer me. I seem possessed by an evil spirit, who persists in dismantling my authenticity—as if demolishing a structure— brick by brick by brick. How can anyone remain alive when dead inside?*

FOUR

As the payday excitement quietened everyone returned to work, though they still yelled greetings and jokes at each other over the grinding roar from the machines. He walked past the workshop chief's office, waving at him cheerfully through the window, while thinking, *Motherfucker has the easiest job in the world, sitting around smoking, having tea and squeezing the women's asses.* Then he moved down the aisle, through a double door, crossed a reception area and entered the Labor Union office.

This visit had become yet another monthly ritual. After the children's illnesses he'd applied to the factory's Labor Union for a Financial Hardship Subsidy. Seven months had passed since, and he was still on the waiting list. He visited the Labor Union office each month to check the status of his claim.

The Labor Union chairman was sitting behind a huge empty desk, smoking and leafing through some newspapers. The tea mug on the desk was still steaming.

How are you, Chairman?

Oh, hello, please sit down, the chairman said, barely lifting his eyes from the newspaper.

So, how's everything?

Good, he said, leaning forward from the edge of the chair.

Working hard?

Oh, yes, he said, lowering his gaze, unsure how to start.

Look, I'm very busy now. Just tell me what I can do for you.

Um, well, it's been another month now, and I'm still waiting . . .

Waiting? Waiting for what?

He was shocked. Oh? Uh . . . waiting for a Financial Hardship Subsidy, that's all.

Oh! Ah! Of course! So sorry about that—I'd forgotten all about it! It's not that I have a bad memory, mind you. It's just that there are so many things that need my attention—every hour of every day—as I'm sure you can understand!

Yes, he said. I won't take up too much of your time. I just wanted to—

I know, I know! I remember the case quite clearly now. Clear as a bell! The chairman stubbed out the cigarette in the ashtray and donned a sympathetic expression.

He said, So, how long, um, how long—roughly—will I still have to wait, then?

Look, my good friend, as I told you before, the Labor Union can only grant Financial Hardship Subsidy to one applicant per month. There are about ten comrades still ahead of you on the waiting list. We work hard every day in accordance with the Party's principles—we do our homework dil-igently, and study every application with great rigor. Believe me, comrade, the applicants ahead of you are—sad to say—in much worse situations than you—So, you see, there's abso-lutely nothing I can do. Your turn will come, I'm sure! The chairman raised his steaming tea mug, blew on it, and took a noisy sip.

In response, he leaned across and offered the chairman a cigarette, plastering a humble smile on his face.

His smile felt every bit as fake as the chirpy sympathy that the chairman conveyed. He suddenly realized that he hadn't smiled sincerely in a very long time.

The chairman blew a perfect blue smoke ring—*he must practice a lot*—and then peered slack-jawed through the smog to admire his dissipating work of art. Then he casually insert-ed his forefinger inside his nostril and started industriously picking, as if fingering delicate sugar in a rose-colored bowl.

He shifted his own gaze to the door, ashamed and re-pulsed, longing to be gone. The air in the office—thickened by smoke—was oppressive, as nauseating as the asking of fa-vors itself. But he took care to prolong his submissive, placa-tory smile, as if eager to hear more.

And so, comrade, as you can see, my hands are tied. I re-ally can't help, even though I greatly wish to. The fact is, I have to be fair to everyone, as I'm sure you'll agree. Look at Lao Sun from your workshop—now, there's a case, if you like!

You know him, I suppose? His mother, wife and two kids all have tuberculosis. His salary is the only source of income for his whole family. Just think, six children! No question, he's in a far worse situation than you. And, guess what, he's been waiting nine months for the subsidy! But what can we do? The chairman paused, sucking on his cigarette deeply, and the ashes dropped on the newspaper. Oops! Never burn a newspaper, he laughed, shaking the ashes onto the floor.

And there are some cases still more pitiful, I believe. I'm the chairman, of course, but there's precious little that even I can do. Look, let me tell you a secret—a secret that's bound to make you feel better. Here is what I recommend. Think about those proletarian brothers and sisters in a worse situation than you—try to have a little empathy—then you'll see how fortunate you are! Trust me on this. Then you'll come to work in much better spirits! The chairman laughed heartily.

Just listen to him! But what else could I expect? The chairman and other higher-ups are all chosen by the Party and are expected to conduct themselves in the interests of the Party, not the interests of the rest of us! They know how to sound high-minded, how to patronize us, how to manipulate, how to insult, how to heckle, how to condescend and—that's it! My sister was right: they're only paid to make our lives miserable. I should have known better than to even try.

It was a familiar pattern of thought. He could never quite understand why he put himself through all this shame and discomfort, just to listen to the same lecture, month after month, how he could collude as his dignity was drained from him, time after time.

He made his escape, and wandered past the reception area, through a door and into the bright sunlit yard. He had—just for the moment—no intention of going back to work. He turned at the corner of the building, and squatted down with his back against the wall, thinking *Another thirty days of waiting.* He hugged his knees with arms crossed, head tilted forward, eyeing the ground as if searching for some precious treasure in the rubble. He envisaged himself—a forlorn silhouette—lost in some derelict neighborhood, muttering to some strangers in an outlandish voice.

If I saw that boy again, I would give him two cents—if I had them. And I'll certainly go and see my sister—not to pay back my debt but to plead to borrow more . . . Thirty days is a very long time.

Since his children's illnesses, he had regularly borrowed money from his sister. He owed her ninety yuan so far, which would take him years to pay back. And he loathed the idea of being beholden to anyone.

Never had he ever imagined that he would live at the mercy of his younger sister—it was he who had taken care of her, after their parents' deaths. He had even delayed his marriage to assist her with college! But since that time, gradually, irrevocably, everything had changed. These days, when he went to assist in his sister's flat, he felt himself to be an impecunious handyman, a relative to be apologized for, a wastrel, someone inextricably, hopelessly, irredeemably in debt. That debt— ninety yuan—that he had racked up in just a few months also seemed to have warped the natural closeness that they used to feel for each other.

Do you need money? She had got into the habit of asking him—almost roughly—often in front of her husband and daughter. Oh, you don't have to tell me, I know. I can tell, just from your face! You just don't want to admit it. Do you? Do you? You know, I can never understand why a man like you can't get a raise. You must just be a really crap worker, is all I can think!

And yet, at other times, she was kinder. Please listen to me, she would say: just listen, big brother, this is what you have to do. You have to talk to your general manager more often, be cheerful, be obliging, build up a personal relationship. You need to get him to like you—maybe visit him on holidays, buy some gifts for him, do him a favor. I'm telling you this for your own benefit. It's the way the world works. You don't understand the world, that's your trouble! Here, take ten yuan. Don't say I never did anything for you: you're my only brother, after all. And besides—she always added this when her husband was there, as if to forestall any later objections—it's just paying you back for those college days, okay? Okay?

He was never sure which hurt more: her kindness or her

barbed tongue, but he accepted both with the same stiff, un-real smile, and only absorbed the sting once he'd departed. For hours afterward, he could still hear her voice yapping in his head, still recall the disdain in her fine eyes. Her words—whether acerbic or consolatory—buzzed continually around his head, like tiny daggers, persistent as insects.

My sister is drifting away from me.

They had never quarreled, except just after their mother's funeral. They had just returned from the crematorium when it had happened. His sister had been sitting cross-legged on their mother's bed, sorting through her belongings, her eyes still fiery from crying. He'd been making tea when he spotted the black-and-white photo on a tall altar table. It shone un-der the warm light of torched candles on a brass candelabra. Surely, their mother?—yet the attractive and stylishly dressed woman in the picture bore no resemblance to their mother they'd just buried.

Where did you find that picture? he had asked, handing her a cup of tea.

At the bottom of the trunk. Mama had hidden it away. I put it up myself. She's so pretty in that picture, isn't she?

She is, he had agreed, trying to remember how his mother looked when he was little. Surely not like that!

I don't know why I'm wasting time on this junk, she'd said, frowning.

Don't waste it, then. She should have trashed those a long

time ago. We should clear all the old junk in this room—once you take whatever you want for yourself, of course.

What are you even talking about? Listen, I live in a college dormitory. I haven't got space for anything! And besides, it's all worthless.

She sold all the valuables to—

I know, I know. To pay for my college, she'd said, setting a stack of folded clothes to one side. Well, these silk Qi Pao may be worth a few yuan at the consignment store.

You take them, he said. Take the candelabra too. That was her favorite.

No space for it . . . Do you plan to marry soon? She'd asked, giving him a sidelong glance.

How can I get married? I can't afford to until you graduate.

Why not? I have less than a year left, after all! I suspect Mama would have wanted you to—although, ever since father left, all she really cared about was when he would die.

Nonsense, he'd said gruffly. She was over him—over all that—years ago.

Over him! How can you be so naïve? How could she ever get over the fact that her husband walked out on her? She hated him till her last gasp! I was there, remember, at her deathbed. Those were the last words she spoke!

Disturbed, he'd stood up and wandered around the room, clasping and unclasping his hands.

Finally he said, He walked out on everyone, even on himself.

Yes, but have you ever asked yourself why?

Why? What do you mean, why?

YOU. He walked out because of you!

What? You're crazy! *I* had nothing to do with it. He never even liked me . . . Remember all the beatings I had—when he seldom laid a finger on you! You're the only one he cared about!

She'd shaken her head. No, no, he concerned himself about your future by far the most—no comparison! Do you really not remember? The very night before he left, when he asked—surely you remember that!

Uh . . . yes. Yes, I do recall it. He asked me what plans I had. And I told him that I wanted to go to the south, find a job, and get married.

And then what happened?

Nothing happened! He said nothing! Absolutely nothing! You were there, at the table. So was Mama.

Her little nostrils had flared. True, he didn't say anything, but he left the very next day. The very day after! Because of you! You were his only son, and he always wanted you to go to college, to train as an engineer, to follow in his footsteps. He was *devastated!* How you disappointed him! How could he continue being alive if he didn't have a hope in hell left?

Right, you can just stop shitting on me right now, he'd snapped. Either you're willfully pretending ignorance or else you're simply blind to the truth. Father was always an adamantine hard-ass. He never recovered after the communists took over and his print shop got nationalized. They even made him work as a typesetter!—that's what broke his spirit. If you think he could deal with his situation you couldn't be more wrong! He was a changed man! In a matter of months—weeks, even—he was drinking more, talking less, beating the fuck out of me! Don't tell me that you don't remember that? Mama could do nothing with him! She was—

Don't you dare blame Mama for his mistakes, she'd screamed. She suffered so much—we *all* did! I can hardly think of him as my father anymore. He didn't even say a proper goodbye!

He'd stood in the middle of the room, both hands jammed in his pockets, helplessly stunned, knowing that she was right.

They had never referred to this argument afterwards; yet, ironically enough, it had somehow cleared the air. In many ways they'd grown closer since until . . . until recently. Until the ninety yuan. Ninety yuan!—it was a terrifying sum. One he sometimes doubted that he could ever repay.

FIVE

He walked along a crumbling concrete road, passing through rows of tin-roofed workshops, from which emerged the constant drone of machinery. He crossed the squalid yard, filled with abandoned machine parts, broken tools and uncoiled wires, rusted from years of rain and wind, until he turned into an asphalt road leading to a bungalow—the so-called Executive building.

In the distance, he could see the glint of a white glass door, dizzyingly bright in the sunlight. The factory clinic too was white—untouchably white—as white as mourning and terrifyingly clean. The moment he stepped inside, he felt as if he was sinking into a cave of endless whiteness. The walls and ceilings were white, the desk, chairs and benches were white, the washbasin and painted drainage pipes were white, the medicine cabinets and the clock above it were white, the curtains and gurney were white, and so were the sheets and pillows. The pregnant doctor wore a loose white robe with white buttons, white sneakers, and a white cap. His heartbeat accelerated, blanketed by such aching whiteness.

What's wrong? the doctor asked. Usually so delicately lovely, she was swollen to twice her normal size, her thick shoulders like scaffolding supporting her neck and head, her features drowned within her broadened face. But her skin glowed with healthy creaminess, and a soft red tinted her cheeks. He'd never seen a woman so over-nourished— her belly looked huge enough to burst. Beside her desk, a white towel shielded bamboo knitting needles and a white, half-knitted, baby sweater.

She was, he believed, about thirty, and had been demobilized to the factory two years ago—a promotion, as she'd been an army nurse and was now a factory doctor. No one knew if she'd been given the correct training. Her husband, an army commander some thirty years her senior, might have had something to do with it.

Workers in the factory frequently gossiped about the doctor and her powerful husband, hissing their latest news as if they were royalty, so far were they removed, in terms of lifestyle, from the factory workers. In the workshops, the canteen, the bathhouse—in every place where people gathered, he was struck by the curiosity that the commander and his wife aroused. Yet every time his foul-mouthed coworkers fantasized about the doctor, he could sense, along with intense excitement, an undertone of envious discontent.

You know they live in a gigantic western-style three-story

mansion, more than 500 square meters, with fifty rooms, a garage, a veranda and much, much more!

Much more of what? Fifty rooms?—don't spin such yarns! And how do you know, anyway: have you been fucking invited?

My neighbor worked in that mansion as a maid, before the liberation. Her master was a textile tycoon who fled the country. That old bitch boasted about that mansion all the time. So, I know more than you do, sucker!

Hey, guys, stop fighting. Just tell me, what is this garage? What's it for?

You're a right fucking idiot, aren't you? A garage is a room for a car. Understand?

Cars need a special room? Wow, it must be a pretty big room!

Bigger than your whole home, moron.

I bet. My home is only five square meters, for six of us. Well, I guess their car needs a room to sleep, fart, and shit too. I would be happy if I could just live in their—in their—what?

Garage, dumbass.

Listen to me, I pass by that place every single day. They have security guards wearing military uniforms, who guard the mansion twenty-four-seven. Those guards stand there for hours like the dead, they don't even blink. Their driver, chef, orderlies and servants—all dressed in army uniform. Shit, it looks like a military barracks!

I know. They have a military jeep and a Soviet car with special license plates—Military 0000 and Military 0001. They could go through all the traffic and the police wouldn't dare to stop them, the motherfuckers. Talk about privilege!

Privilege! Wow, that's a damn big word for someone like you.

Privilege? Let me tell you what's privilege. The damn white shoes that the doctor wears! That's fucking privilege! I dare you to wear white shoes in this shithole. I dare every one of you! Look at your shoes, all of you. They're all black and coarse, torn and sticky, but she wears clean white shoes. We get soaked in stinking machine oil but the commander's jeep drops her off for work right in front of the Executive Building. And then she sits in that white room, wearing clean white shoes all year long—doing nothing but farting and knitting and making more than all ten of us put together! *That's* privilege!

Hey, you forgot her electric fan. We sweat, wet to the bone during summer—must be forty degrees in this shithole—and she gets an electric fan in her little white room. The only electric fan in the whole factory! No, wait, I take that back. The general manager has one. My kids don't even know what an electric fan is. I had to draw them a picture.

Stop fucking bullshitting! You don't even know how to write, so how can you draw a picture? With your feet?

Listen, dickhead, if I'd been allowed an education, I could

have been an artist and not have to hang around here with an asshole like you.

I had a row with my wife before the Spring Festival. She told me that she wanted a pair of white sneakers. I said, fuck you bitch, white sneakers? Who do you think you are? The doctor? If your pussy was as good as the doctor's, you'd have married a commander, not a penniless member of the proletariat. White shoes? White shoes? Dream on! And you know what? The fucking bitch refused to talk to me for a week!

There was an outburst of laughter.

Do you guys know that every Spring Festival, our general manager pays a visit, just to lick the commander's boots and to fawn on his bitch? Every time he sees the doctor, he says, Oh, doctor, you look as gorgeous as ever! I'm fucking sick of it.

Well, she *is* rather gorgeous.

Shit, if she wasn't pretty, do you think that the commander would have married her? God knows how many times the fucker's been married!

Tell you what: our general manager uses her husband's army ration-card to buy beef every month.

No! No way! How can you know that?

The manager made a slip of the tongue the other day at the canteen. I overheard it.

People like them live completely different lives, don't they? Fuck, yes! But our general manager himself is nobody compared to the commander.

If the general manager is nobody, then what are we?

We're lumps of mud, clods, insects, worms, roaches, ants and flies—we're crocks of shit, we're piles of crap—that's all we are. That's why we are stuck in this filthy shithole. Smell your fucking hands, then you'll see the truth!

All this ran through his brain as he sat in the white wooden chair, eyeing the doctor's white raiment. He had rarely had any contact with the doctor—he couldn't afford to be sick—but he found himself fascinated by those smooth white shoes. He thought, *Xiao Ming was right: the shoes tell the tale. The shoes worn by those with power, influence and privilege single them out. Those shoes never meant to touch the dusty streets— they're destined to walk higher up, above the streets, the buildings, the factories, the ordinary crowds, above the city itself!*

What's wrong? The doctor repeated her question, with neither impatience nor interest.

I'm dizzy, he replied, breaking free from his trance and glancing, from the corner of his eye, at the clock on the wall. Her clock was at least a half-hour faster than the one in the workshop. *But which was correct? If only time could be manipulated to move, sometimes faster, sometimes slower!*

The doctor motioned for him to sit on a bench. While she took his blood pressure, he glimpsed her dimpled pretty hands and fingers and tried to imagine what kind of food she and her husband ate: dumplings, seafood, beef, chicken, voluptuous feasts . . . The well-off, well-nourished, sixty-something Commander must have a healthy sex life to have made his young wife pregnant—that alone was an incomparable privilege.

He thought about his own wife, her cracked and work-worn hands, and recalled the last time that they had sex—a warm night, months ago. It was shortly after that when he first noticed the bald patch on his head and—coincidentally—quite a few surprising gray strands on his wife's. Of course, neither of these alterations could have happened overnight: basically, they were both worn-out.

Hmm. Blood pressure is a little high. You just got paid, didn't you? the doctor joked, while signing his sick note. He had of course just been paid, but he could find nothing amusing about it. The clean, crisp whiteness seemed to add a deadly chill to the room. He felt unpleasantly cold, as if grappling with a shock of grief. Glancing at the doctor's rosy, mocking face, he forced a polite smile and lowered his gaze. *She could knit a baby sweater during work hours—even take a nap on the gurney, if she wanted to. No one would ever dare to stop her. If she applied for a Financial Hardship Subsidy—which is laughable, of course—the Chairman of the Labor Union would instantly approve it, no matter how many people were on the waiting list. Both the General Manager and the Chairman of the Labor Union would succumb to her influence, especially as the ears and eyes of the Commander are supposed to be everywhere.*

The doctor removed a small paper bag—six centimeters

wide and nine centimeters long—from the desk drawer, heaved herself to her feet and carefully smoothed down the wrinkles on her clothes. At the medicine cabinet, she selected a glass bottle and counted some white tablets into the bag.

He returned dizzily to the workshop, clutching his sick-note and the paper bag. It was lunch-hour: the workshop was empty, as everyone had departed to the canteen. He sat down heavily on a bench, plagued by the resonant aura of machine oil, confused by the excesses of his imagination.

Doctors could kill people, he thought, enamel mug in one hand, white tablet in the other. The white tablet in his hand metamorphosed into the doctor's face—pink-flushed, plump, its features blurred, somehow expressionless. *My younger daughter takes a white tablet every day for pleurisy, as does my son for nephritis—and here is another white tablet, for high blood pressure. All these tablets—perhaps she's given me the wrong one?—all these white tablets! To cure or to kill?*

So many transparent glass bottles in the clinic's medicine cabinet, each labeled with a sticker no bigger than a thumb-nail, the words on each thumbnail as small and wriggly as ants. The doctor had chosen the glass bottle and poured out the tablets without even seeming to check the label.

Had it been the right bottle? What if the bottle had been mislabeled? Her mind was probably more focused on knitting that soft sweater for her baby.

He stared at the white tablet in his hand, hesitating. People could die from diseases, or from taking the wrong medicine. He caressed the smooth white tablet, as if some foreteller of his fate, seeking reassurance from its smooth whiteness.

Finally, he swallowed it.

SIX

He was passing some shops on the way home when he saw a familiar figure leaving a bakery, a pretty cookie tin in his hand. He slowed down and dismounted by the curbside.

Hello.

Oh, hello, his brother-in-law said, as if surprised.

Do you have a day off?

No, I'm on the way home to pick up my suitcase. I only stopped to buy some walnut cookies for Lulu.

The particular tenderness in his tone when mentioning Lulu stirred him. He smiled and asked: Heading out of town again?

Yes.

For how long?

A week. So, what's up with you?

I took sick leave today.

What's the matter?

Just high blood pressure.

Hmm. Since when?

Since this morning. But I have pills.

The brother-in-law tucked the tin under an arm and offered him a cigarette. Here, try this.

He did not refuse. Two cigarettes were lit by the same match: they both squatted on their heels next to his bicycle. With a sidelong glance, he noticed the cookie tin was painted with pink peony blossoms. *This cigarette costs thirty-five cents a pack—mine only eight cents. And he bought walnut cookies for Lulu—who will probably show the tin to my daughters once all the cookies are eaten. This fellow lives well.*

He'd always found his brother-in-law likable. In fact, they got along perfectly well, and when they drank together, he'd even found that they could share thoughts with each other. But there was still something about him that caused him to feel self-conscious—something that, from time to time, tempted him to biting intent.

You're coming to our house this Sunday? his brother-in-law asked.

No. Does anything need to be fixed?

Sorry, I mean, if you have time, please come. Our armoire mirror is broken.

How did that happen?

A broken mirror is very dangerous, his brother-in-law continued. I'd hate for Lulu to get cut or something.

Don't worry. I'll get it fixed.

His brother-in-law seemed encumbered, somehow. He

peered at him through the haze of smoke, thinking that he didn't look particularly well. His cheeks were sallow and splotched with liver spots, his throat looked slack, his eyes yellowish.

Was it an accident? he asked suddenly, surprising himself.

What?

The broken mirror.

Uh . . . she threw a tea mug, his brother-in-law said, averting his gaze. They watched a young woman pass with a child wagon, chatting to the child in a singsong voice.

That tea mug. Was it about the housing allotment?

It's always about something, his brother-in-law said glumly.

My sister is desperate to move out of that neighborhood.

She certainly is. Who isn't? But what can she expect? I'm working as hard as I can to make it happen, but my submission is rejected, over and over again! She doesn't care anymore and nor do I. He stabbed his cigarette hard into the dirt . . . But I do care about Lulu. It upsets her, seeing us fight.

What's the use of you two fighting if they rejected your submission? That's not going to make them accept it!

Tell your sister! Listen, Lulu didn't even say goodbye to me before she left for school. And I forgot to tell her that I was leaving today. That's why I bought her these.

Once again he heard the tenderness in his tone whenever Lulu was mentioned.

His brother-in-law held out his cigarette pack to him and said: Here, take this.

No, keep it, I don't want your cigarettes.

Just take it, his brother-in-law said, pushing the pack into his hand. Much obliged to you for taking care of that mirror.

He smiled back but said nothing.

His brother-in-law walked heavily away. After a few steps, he turned around and questioned, I always did my damn best, didn't I? Well? Didn't I?

Yes, you did, he said.

Right. Go tell your sister.

He followed the retreating figure with his eyes, murmuring *We all did our damn best.*

As he wheeled his bicycle home, he spotted Xiao Ma leaning against his door, smoking. Xiao Ma had recently broken his arm at work and still wore a splint.

Hello, brother, Xiao Ma greeted him. Why back so early?

Sick leave. My blood pressure's a little high.

You didn't have that before, did you? Xiao Ma said, looking concerned.

No, I haven't even had sick leave for almost ten years.

How'd you find out?

I just felt a little dizzy. My systolic pressure's above 180.

Whoa, that's very high! You've got to be careful. You'd better rest.

Yet Xiao Ma still blocked his way, as if he had more to communicate.

He couldn't help noticing that the white splint looped around Xiao Ma's neck had turned agate grey. *Had it been over-washed, or allowed to get dirty?*

How long will you have to wear that splint? he asked.

About another month—it's awkward as shit. There's stuff at home I can't fix.

I can give you a hand, if you need it.

No, no, you've got high blood pressure. Anyway, it's not urgent, Xiao Ma said, offering him a cigarette. He refused it.

What's not urgent? he asked, for something to say.

Oh, no big deal, just a light fixture. When you feel a little better it'd be great if you helped me change it over.

You mean from a bulb to a fluorescent one?

Exactly. My wife's been fussing about it until I can't stand it anymore.

Well, fluorescent's brighter. Saves electricity too.

I know, I know. I've bought everything required, Xiao Ma said, offering him a cigarette again. As it seemed rude to refuse twice, he accepted it, and Xiao Ma lit it, adding, we could have a drink too.

The doctor said that I shouldn't drink, he said gloomily.

Oh, well, we won't overdo it. Just a couple of drinks can't hurt.

It was strange, the thought. *They both seemed more re-*

laxed, just at the mere mention of drinking . . . All right. I'll fix the light and we'll enjoy a couple of drinks, he said suddenly. Maybe Sunday.

It was a common request for him, as he enjoyed the reputation, throughout Worker Village, of being a handyman. Day in and day out he made himself useful: assisting with housework, changing light fixtures, installing stoves, fixing bicycles, building kitchen shacks, plastering walls, repairing roofs, or mending pots, pans, and water buckets. Whenever he was sent for he'd get the work done. Knowing that he enjoyed a drink, his neighbors might buy him some liquor in return—which he'd take care to share with the man of the family. Yet, he never received pecuniary compensation for his good nature—had never even thought about it.

For this reason, during the Spring Festival, grateful neighbors and colleagues took turns to visit his home—some even invited him to dinner. He enjoyed the Spring Festival, relishing the stream of people taking the time to come to his house—almost a pilgrimage—to praise his skills, his deftness and his good nature. At these times a flame of pride and satisfaction flared inside him, as though he had surfaced from out of the choking mud in which he generally felt mired. For a few days, at least, he would hold his head high and walk through Worker Village with a tipsy and joyous solemnity, his debts and failures forgotten.

But the Spring Festival seemed a long time ago as he

trudged home. His wife looked shocked as he pushed open the door.

What, back so early? Are you all right? She was perched on a stool, sewing a quilt for his sister. Cotton fluff adhered to her hair and clothes, like fragments of cloud. Their son and younger daughter napped peacefully on the other side of the room.

My blood pressure's a little high, so the doctor sent me home. As he sat down, he automatically removed his pay packet and tossed it on the table. For some reason—the cigarette?—he felt slightly giddy again.

Carefully pinning her needle to the front of her jacket, she took possession of the precious envelope, her fingers skimming through the thin stack of banknotes, counting, the speed of her fingers making him feel sicker. Then she went to the cupboard and removed a scrap of paper from a drawer, murmuring: Ten yuan for grain; two yuan for rent; five yuan for coal, firewood, water and electricity; five yuan for debt to Aunt Liu; six yuan for milk; ten yuan for eggs and meat— that's thirty-eight. Only thirty yuan here—not enough for the month. Not to mention cooking oil . . . She sighed, and added, Here. For you.

She gave him two yuan and seventy-five cents each month, which he spent on cigarettes and the occasional lunch, because he couldn't afford the factory canteen every day. Silently, he pocketed the money.

Another tough month! she said, forcing a wan little smile. Do you want to eat something? You forgot your lunch again.

No, I'm not at all hungry. But why do you owe Aunt Liu five yuan?

I borrowed it for my sister. You know how she's been wanting to change her job for a long time. Anyway, she begged and begged, and at last her workshop chief promised to arrange it, so she wanted to buy two bottles of liquor as a gift for him. Unluckily neither of us had enough, so I borrowed five yuan from Aunt Liu.

If she wants to buy her workshop chief a gift, that's her own damn business, he said, shaking his head. Why should *you* borrow money for her? Doesn't she know our kids are sick?

Ah!—but you know my sister! Her life is hard and she's too shy to ask anyone else for help. She came two days ago, bringing a bag of candy for the kids. Then she just sat there, hesitating and blushing for the longest time . . . And besides, I'm her only sister, and she's promised to pay me back next payday. Oh, and Aunt Liu has recommended me for a babysitting job! A couple with a newborn—they wanted to pay six yuan a month, but they've agreed to eight. That starts in two weeks.

He hardly heard her. His eye was suddenly captured by the slant of afternoon sun on the quilt: a silky dark green brocade with metallic plum blossoms. Through the window stood the boundless sky, the puffed clouds shifting between blue and gray, gray and blue. The quilt seemed to glitter in the shaft of light, as if the clouds themselves were scudding across its silvery surface.

Then he snapped out of his daze, recalling the ninety yuan that he owed his sister. *How could his wife have failed to mention that?*

Not enough for the month was all she'd said.

Not enough for the month, indeed!

To her surprise, he stood up sharply and left the room, heading swiftly toward the shack.

SEVEN

*N*ot *enough for the month. Not enough for the month.* The words nibbled at him like gnats as he lay down and covered himself with a cotton quilt. Closing his eyes, he imagined the green quilt, tall and heavy as a wall, pressing against his chest, bearing down on him, the breaths oozing out of him, smothering him deeper with each gasp.

This smothering is what debt feels like, he thought. He tried to imagine something else, but each subject oiled its way back to the first. It colored everything, encompassed everything. He recalled the previous Sunday, when his niece Lulu had been sent with a message from his sister.

Jiu Jiu[4], I'm afraid our windowpane's broken again, Lulu had said, flashing that winning smile.

With a groan, he'd collected the materials he needed and set off for his sister's.

His sister lived on the first floor of a four-story apartment building, its windows facing a backyard. As the neighborhood children used this as a playground—deploying sling-

---

4 Jiu Jiu: *uncle* in Chinese, the mother's brother.

shots and kicking balls as well as throwing stones—the windows on that side naturally took the brunt of any trouble. Also, his sister was constantly quarreling and stirring up arguments with her neighbors, immersing herself in bitter vexations, with the result that her windows suffered even more than all the rest.

It occurred to him that young Lulu's philosophy was more realistic than her mother's.

We're not the only family with broken windows. It was an accident. It just—happens, he'd heard her remark, with that entrancing laugh. And perhaps it really had been an accident, on this occasion, as some of those children were her friends. Yet replacing his sister's smashed windowpanes remained part of his routine, in season and out of season, all year round.

His sister had been vigorously washing clothes in a basin when he arrived. Her first comment had been a complaint that she'd wasted hours banging on neighbors' doors without securing a confession from the vandal concerned. He'd sensed hostility in every inch of her, and had clamped his mouth shut, to avoid adding fuel to the flames.

Finally, she was tired of the subject, asking, So, where's Lulu?

She wanted to stay at my home and play.

Lulu was his sister's only child. After her birth, she had endured several miscarriages, after which she'd been declared unable to conceive. Despite this, she'd spent years taking

traditional Chinese fertility medicine—continually object-
ing that it made her feel tired and heavy—yet refused to stop
trying. It seemed that, the older she grew the more obsessed
and impatient she became with her infertility. These days she
tended to lose her temper with no good reason, to become
extraordinarily upset over nothing, and to be constantly in a
sour mood. He secretly wondered whether Chinese medicine
might not be to blame.

She wanted to play, did she? his sister repeated, frowning.
Well! I only hope that she'll be back before dusk. It's not safe
for anyone to walk in the dark alone. A girl was raped in a
nearby alley just a week ago.

How on earth did that happen?

Simple. She went to the public bathhouse, was returning home in the dark and was seized. She was at Lulu's
own school.

Did they arrest the fellow?

No. Unfortunately, the girl was too terrified to remember
much—except that he had a mustache, which is no help at all,
she said, curling her lip. Our Community Committee keeps
urging people to suppress this so-called rumor—far too late,
of course! Instantly, everyone's tongues were wagging, soil-
ing the poor creature's family name. Even the teachers at
school—just dramatizing the situation! Her parents felt so
humiliated that they've sent her away to the countryside. The

girl is barely nine years old and her life is finished—but you can imagine how I've worried about Lulu, ever since!

I'll make sure she gets home before dark, he soothed her. Then, anxious to get on, he slipped on a pair of old cotton gloves, stepped onto the windowsill, squatted down, and started brushing up the broken glass.

How many times have you done this recently? she demanded.

When he, still thinking about that girl and her family, missed this, she raised her voice and asked again. Baffled, he cleared his throat, wondering what she meant by *recently*. One month? Three months? He was always doing it!

I—can't remember. The windowsill was almost two meters above the ground, and very narrow. Below him, shattered glass scintillated in the sunlight, while his body seemed almost hanging in midair. It seemed to him—uncanny thought—that his silhouette too was jagged, incomplete, less than whole. *So many things in life could be so easily and unexpectedly broken, just like glass.*

You can't remember? What's wrong with you? she accused, tucking her hair behind her ears with a hand still lathered with soap, fire burning in her eyes. Her snappiness jarred on him.

I just don't remember. If I had to guess, I'd say, maybe the second time in a month.

You're getting more and more like my husband: he often pretends that he can't remember anything, just to frustrate me! Now you're just the same. You really can't remember how many times you've come over in a month? Really? Really?

Although her harsh voice was muffled by the splash of the water and the sound of fierce scrubbing he breathed in every word, thinking *She's simply trying to antagonize me so I don't come back. I don't know how she sees me these days, but definitely not as a big brother. She certainly doesn't respect me anymore. I've been coming to change the broken glass here for at least seven years, perhaps twice a month: that's one hundred and seventy times. I've done it willingly and for free. I've done her house chores for free, too. Now she probably thinks I'm only helping because I needed to borrow her money—just listen to her, moaning, complaining, venting!—but all I can do is to turn a deaf ear, to let her take it out on me, to just get the work done. I owe her money, after all.*

Yet he couldn't help remembering how, over the years, he and his sister had shared moments of anxiety, helplessness, bitterness, and sweetness together.

He recalled the time during the Great Famine in 1960 when his sister had stolen two dried steamed buns from a government canteen, crumpled them in her undershirt and brought them to his home; the time he'd bribed the director of the general affairs department with a bottle of liquor in order to access a ration stamp for two canvas trunks for his sister's dowry; the time he and his wife had prepared and cooked for two solid days for his sister's wedding banquet, and finally gone home—drunk and hungry, but extraordinarily happy. There was also that time when his wife experienced dystocia, and his sister—heavily pregnant herself—had waited with him in the hospital for fifteen hours, until her hand must have ached from the pain of his grip.

When he remembered all this, he couldn't understand what had happened between them, only that something had changed, that something irredeemably precious had slipped away. The mere thought made his spine twinge, as though he'd been kicked at the base of it.

While he was absorbed, his sister started again: It's an outrage, the little pricks we have in this neighborhood! They only broke my window this time but—you wait, you just wait. One day they'll sneak in and steal from us, just mark my words. Vicious and vulgar, they run around like homeless cats and dogs. Their parents toss them onto the street like garbage, turning a blind eye to everything they do. Our damn neighbors turn my stomach. Men, women—makes no difference—they're all the same: coarse, uncultured, caustic, sinister, self-righteous asses! They fight over the communal spaces, only to fill them up with rubbish! They dump sludge in the tap trough and clog the entire drainage system! You'd be amazed to know how many people in this flat don't even flush their toilets! To be honest, I'd prefer that Lulu had no contact with any of the children here, but there's only so much that I can do when she has to attend the same school. Heaven knows how long I've wanted to move out of this hellhole!

While his sister's acidity was still smoldering, he'd taken off his gloves and started to calculate. The glass was 30 x 30 centimeters, and he'd need sixty centimeter-long nails to embed the new glass into the window frame. The distance between each nail was exactly two centimeters. He dispatched each nail neatly, mechanically, without thought.

Are you listening to me? his sister asked sharply.

Yes, yes.

Then why don't you ever say anything? We're the only ones here. I don't want to talk to a stick!

Well, I think you should move away, he said, after a moment. You could have moved a long time ago. He spoke rather louder than usual to prove that she'd got his attention.

You're telling me! But where? You don't know how many times we've quarreled over this shitty flat! No private kitchen, no toilet—everything ugly, dim and dreary—and the disgusting neighbors only make it worse. It's not fit for a dog! And I'll tell you this: my husband's clumsy not only with his hands but with his brain, too. I've had about enough. If it wasn't for Lulu, I'd divorce him and go live by myself!

He was shocked. He thought she was longing for another baby, not a divorce! But he smiled, without the slightest censure, and fell silent.

His sister took his support for granted, saying bitterly, He hands in his application for housing allotment every year and gets rejected every single time. I keep telling him that he has to do something to get it—but he never listens! It's as if he *enjoys* muddling along, somehow. He must know by now that it's impossible to maneuver a housing allotment application without some special relationships with the higher-ups—but vying for favors seems to be an unachievable skill: one either has it—or one doesn't! And he certainly doesn't! Anyway, they will announce this year's housing allotment result next week. Heaven knows what will happen this time. I'm exhausted from nagging him. I've had just about enough. She released a sigh of sullen contempt.

Well, he's a rather reserved man, he ventured, hammering his last nail.

Reserved? Reserved? You don't have to be tactful with me!—It's just fear, fear and laziness! You're both of you so reserved that you forget that children need to eat!—oh, I never could understand men! She stood up, drying her hands vigorously with a small towel, and adding, as an afterthought: Would you like a cup of tea?

No, thank you, he said, not looking up, sealing the edge of the windowpane with paste and the putty knife. She poured a cup for herself, holding the teacup in her hand and watching him. He saw concern in her eyes, along with something else that he couldn't read.

As she sipped, she said: I would never wish to meddle in

your family affairs, brother. But as you *are* my brother, I feel obliged to tell you the truth. I sometimes worry that you're simply too naïve and impractical, just like my husband. Do you really imagine that you'll ever get a raise without patronage from your workshop chief or some higher leader in your factory? If so, then you're crazy! They make your life hard, don't they? Well, that's what they're paid to do! You should have figured that out a long time ago, with two sickly kids and an unemployed spouse! Oh, don't get me wrong. I know how hard it must be for five of you to exist on your own salary. I don't even mind loaning you money—as long as I have any, that is. But really, you could try a little harder! Pay a visit to the homes of your general manager or the Chairman of the Labor Union, taking a nice gift! Go to the Community Committee in Worker Village and ask them to find your wife a job! Just do *something!*

She dragged out the last word as if trying to bring it to his attention, her eyes almost blazing at him.

Her tone, with its undertone of veiled contempt, stayed with him, needling him, just under the surface of his thoughts, until the moment when he lay wakeful in bed. Then his sister's bitter, burning words curdled like spoiled milk in his mind. He thought, *Life isn't living anymore—but, it's only a long, resigned period of waiting for something better, something that will probably never happen.*

EIGHT

Another payday. Accountant Liu walked over and handed him an envelope. He couldn't wait to count the banknotes.

Forty yuan and seventy-five cents—ten yuan more.

It couldn't be right. It must be wrong! Wrong! he exclaimed soundlessly. Wetting his finger with spittle, he counted it twice more. He was correct—forty yuan and seventy-five cents. He put the money and the pay slip into his pocket and started pacing in front of the tool racks, utterly distracted. The furry stain on the concrete floor looked darker, though as greasy as ever. The sight of it—as so often—disturbed him.

He sat on the stool in the corner of the workshop, lit a cigarette and spat out a wad of tobacco leaves, biting his lips feverishly. He noticed Xiao Yang wandering toward the toilet again: though it wasn't even lunchtime yet, he'd already gone three times. The old wall-clock seemed dead. He noticed these things with a kind of desperation, clutching at normality. *He wasn't dreaming—or was he?* He took out the money, cigarette jutting from his mouth, counting it again.

So strange!—ten yuan more. They would never give me a raise without telling me, surely? Perhaps Accountant Liu made a mistake and gave me extra accidentally? Yet Liu—astute, meticulous, prudent—never made a mistake. And, if he had, just this once, he would certainly discover it and track it down. *In such a case, if I kept the money and denied it, Liu could even lose his job . . .*

Fingering the notes, he thought, *Ten yuan can last a while and buy a lot of things, maybe some meat and eggs from the black market. The kids would be thrilled! Or perhaps I should give the ten yuan to my sister, in part-payment of my debt?*

Just then he spotted Accountant Liu, smiling at him. His hands began to tremble.

Ten yuan extra, right? Liu spoke lightly, a sly look on his face.

Ah, L-L-Liu, he stammered.

It's a raise, ten yuan a month, starting next month, Liu said. We have not forgotten about you, my friend.

So: thirty yuan had finally become forty. He nodded, almost dizzy. *Liu mentioned we—but who did he mean by we?*

This particular extra ten yuan is from me. I know how much you need it, Liu said, in a lowered tone. Just between ourselves, if you please! I do have some petty cash, you know. It's all right: you can always pay me back. No big deal! And listen, that's not all!—your application for the Financial Hardship Subsidy was also approved. You should get another ten next month from that. The chairman of the Labor Union told me, only yesterday.

Thirty had turned into forty; forty had turned into fifty. The *next-month* mantra had finally worked! Tentative as he was by nature, he couldn't suppress a great bounding sense of hope.

He was just beginning to express his thanks when Liu stopped smiling. His face suffused with sudden rage, he hissed, I did this for you! Only for you, you motherfucker! You forced me to steal! I jeopardized my job for you!

I'm so sorry—so sorry—I never intended—I never . . . Terrified and shaken, he rolled from side to side. A gentle shaking woke him, his wife's face looming whitely above.

Are you all right? she asked, concern in her tone.

He blinked dizzily.

Eh . . . eh . . . what? Yes, yes, I'm fine.

I'm glad, she said. It's almost three thirty. You need to get going! Please buy some flour from the grain shop. We've had corn buns for several days now and the kids want noodles for dinner.

And with this, she neatly stacked ten yuan, their grain ration card and a flour sack on the table beside the bed. While she caught the sight of the cigarette pack on the table, she grimaced slightly.

You didn't buy that cigarette yourself, did you? Her voice so clear, so achingly sharp, with a touch of mock-reproval.

No, he said brusquely. Someone gave it to me.

She caught something malevolent in his tone, and rapidly changed the subject. I saw Grandma Chen at the tap, she said. She was carrying her water in a cooking pot. Her water-bucket's leaking, and she was wondering if you might be able to repair it.

I'll see what I can do, he said mechanically.

Do you still feel dizzy?

Just a little.

I can go with you if you like.

No, no, you stay with the kids, he said, pocketing the ration card and money. *How strange he felt!*

And while you're at the grain shop, see if they've got any more rice. The girls have been longing for rice for a while.

All right.

Still dazed, he thought, *Could Accountant Liu really give me extra ten yuan? Is that possible? He mentioned petty cash, but that—surely—belongs to the factory. But I suppose Liu has plenty of cash in his drawer. He could probably give me twenty yuan if he wanted!*

He took out a small ball of hemp rope from the table drawer and grabbed the things his wife had set on the table. As he strode outside to his bicycle, he could almost hear banknotes rustling in his ears.

NINE

The grain shop, made from heavy concrete slabs, stood on the roadside corner like a fortress. The wooden doors were reinforced with double panels and two iron locks, and the threshold beam above the steps was almost a foot high. Three bare bulbs on dusty cords dangled from the ceiling, casting thin shadows over the gunnysackss piled behind the counter. A male clerk shuttled between the counter and the gunnysackss, the shadows of the bulbs swaying with his movements. He looked weary and dusty, as if perpetually deprived of sunlight. There was also a black cat, sleek, subtly contemptuous, stretched along the sacks.

Customers queued along the wall that led to the payment window, afterwards they collected the grain from the clerk at the little counter. The grain shop was infested with rats, and the odor of decayed droppings was strong. The cat was kept in order to catch the rodents, but no cat in the world could have caught them all.

He stood in the queue a long time before reaching the window, watching the cat patrolling the gunnysacks. It seemed to be watching him: its eerie, yellowish eyes almost boring into him. Chilled, he turned around—yet still sensing those eyes glued on his back, drilling into him from the gunnysacks.

A pudgy woman squatted at a desk in the payment window. She wore a white cap similar in style to the factory doctor's but both wrinkled and filthy. All he could see of her was flabby cheeks, droopy eyelids, flaccid hands. He removed the grain ration card from his pocket and handed it to her.

She thumbed through the pages, sliding her thick fingers up and down her abacus beads. Then she scribbled down a number and stamped his card.

Nine yuan! she yelled hoarsely.

He delved into his pocket and retrieved a two-yuan bill. But he needed his ten-yuan bill. He scrabbled desperately in his pocket, finding only seventy-five cents. Two yuan and seventy-five cents: his pocket money. Was that all he had?

His hand flew back to his other pocket. *Where was the ten-yuan bill?* He felt a sudden panicky acceleration in his pulse. His hands skittered through all his pockets—jacket, pants, undershirt—but found nothing beyond a half-pack of cigarettes and a matchbox. He laid the two yuan and seventy-five cents, the cigarette pack and the matchbox on the ledge and scoured the floor, sick with fear. His throat was burning, his temples throbbed, his hands probed his pockets, over and over again.

Nine yuan! The woman rasped, louder, as if he was deaf.

Hurry up! We're all waiting, someone in the queue growled. This encouraged the rest. (Move! Get on with it! Why so slow?) Nine yuan! Can't you hear? the woman hissed.

I—I can't find the money. It was in my pocket, but somehow it's gone. It's gone!

Then step aside! Look at the queue. They're all waiting, just for you! Can't you hear? I told you, step aside! the woman said. She hastily scratched the number off on the ration card and threw it at him, snapping, Next!

Dazed, he collected his flour sack, money, cigarette pack, match box and ration card, and withdrew. On his way out, he humbly asked everyone in the queue if they'd seen his money. His tone was imploring. He knew most of them: he had helped them with chores, attended Community Committee meetings with them, worked with them across the factory floor. Yet today they seemed to look at him strangely, almost averting their eyes, as if disbelieving him.

As he turned to leave the grain shop, he heard the cat leap down behind him. He paused, caught his foot on the threshold and stumbled. Grasping hold of the door frame to stop himself from falling, he lurched down the steps.

Mew . . . ew . . . eow!

Even the cat sounded derisive. Shocked, he swayed outside the grain shop, still tightly gripping his flour sack and ration card. He felt the sunlight crack through him, raking away everything with the exception of his intense dream—the dream about payday, Accountant Liu, his raise, the Financial Hardship Subsidy, the extra ten yuan. Only the dream seemed real, in his mind. Then the ten-yuan bill, strangely magnified, arose in his consciousness, and twisted, turning, warping, inverting itself, before it slipped away.

He had held ten yuan in his hand. He had *held* it. Where was it now, though? It was gone—and that was that.

Half-blinded by the shock of sunlight, he shook his head oddly, almost humming to himself. A strange little smile appeared—a simple smile, not sad yet somehow empty, as if he was puzzling to identify a stray thought from something.

Leaving his bicycle propped outside the grain shop, he walked dazedly along the same route he had taken. His gaze swept both sides of the street, from left to right, right to left, back and forth. Occasionally he stooped, sifted through a few dry leaves, dirt or debris, then stumbled forward again, muttering to himself, half-slurring his words, as if tipsy.

The nearer he got to his home, the more agitated he became and the more often he stopped to scrabble through detritus. At last, he stopped altogether and acknowledged the truth: he could not look his wife in the eye and admit something that he himself couldn't face. Defeated, he turned around and fumbled his way back toward the grain shop.

From time to time, he was greeted by neighbors, or by others who knew him. Smiling dimly, he hardly heard what they said. Yet a strange, pathetic, unstoppable voice inside his head demanded to be heard, pushing him into an ever-deeper panic. He would say: Have you seen any money on the street? I lost ten yuan, just a little while ago. I lost it here, on this street (he raised his hands to the sky, waving, as if he was swearing). Did you see it? Ten yuan. A single bill. It's all our food money for this month, yet— in the blink of an eye—it's gone! On this street. Money for our food. I need to buy flour, my wife wants to make noodles. My kids want noodles for dinner. On this very street—just like that! A single bill. For noodles. Ten yuan, yes, ten yuan!

The whining voice went on and on, repeating the same words to anyone who would listen, gripping the arms of passersby he didn't even know. As he talked, he continually fumbled in his pockets, turning them inside out, as if for confirmation. (In this pocket, this pocket here . . .)

At one point he found himself in the middle of the street, rows of houses bearing down upon him from either side, exhausted, humiliated, covered in sweat; and yet that voice—it seemed no longer his own—inflamed, verbose, hopeful— would not give up.

What astounded him was that someone could talk so tirelessly and so desperately about one simple happening, especially when that *someone* was some version of himself. His river of words finally wore out his listeners as he clomped his way back to the grain shop. But one man took pity on him and stopped, interrupting him, drawing him aside and asking, Are you all right?

Ah, yes, yes, yes, he said. I'm all right. Eh . . . I'm just looking for a ten-yuan bill. I lost it somewhere here. It's our food money for this month, you know. For flour—for noodles. It's gone, from my pocket, this pocket, here. Ten yuan—a single note! A single note!

He couldn't recall the man's name, though he knew that he lived in Worker Village. He had once helped him with a roof repair and they'd shared a drink together—or perhaps they hadn't? It disturbed him that he couldn't quite remember.

Just go home now, it's getting late, the man advised, concern in his voice.

No, no, I have to find the money. A single—and flour, for noodles. I have to find the money and buy flour. It's our money for the whole—

The grain shop will be closed by this time, the man said, not unkindly. The money's lost. If you can't find it, you can't find it. What else can you do?

What else can I do? he repeated, raising his voice and glaring at the man.

Well, said the man reluctantly, I suppose you could report it to the police, if you think it was stolen.

The police? Ah, no. No, I don't need the police. Besides, it wasn't stolen. I lost it. A single note, ten yuan. It's somewhere

here on the street—I have to find it. A single note, a single—he said, shaking his head.

You'd do better to listen to me. Listen, it's getting late. Just go home.

How can I go home? I have to find my money. It's here, he said, his fingers randomly pointing to the ground.

The man sighed and walked away.

It's not stolen. I lost it. You hear me?! I lost it! he shouted after him, but the man did not turn around.

He continued staggering along the street, hunching down now and then, rambling and talking to himself.

As evening drew in and the streetlights came on, a rough-looking stranger in his early thirties came along on a bicycle. The fellow screamed at him rudely, as if they were old acquaintances, though he had never seen him before.

Hey, brother! Time to go home. You've been looking for that damn money all afternoon like a fucking idiot. Can't you understand? Your money's gone! It's either lost or stolen. Doesn't matter. Anyway, it's gone. Gone! Gone! Gone! Damn it, can't you hear me?! You're just making a fucking idiot out of yourself!

His eyes reddening, he yelled back: You're the damn fool! It's my money. It's our fucking *food* money! But—but—but the money's gone. I lost it. I lost our food money. And you—you—you just mind your own damn business!

You're an idiot. No one will ever return dropped money. It's gone for good!

Motherfucker! he muttered, as the man mounted his bicycle and rode off into the gathering shadows. He very seldom swore, and found it strangely satisfying. Fucking busybody! You know shit. I'll never help you with a repair, not even if you beg me!

But then worry started pawing at him again.

After all, he's right. No one will return money, even if it's found. No one! And if it was stolen . . .

The word *stolen* suddenly struck him. Stolen!

In fact, the rude fellow was probably right. It really could have been stolen. Snapping out of his trace, he stopped in the middle of the street. *Yes, stolen! Why didn't I think of this before? Someone stole that ten yuan right out of my pocket!*

Suddenly he remembered his bicycle.

Dropping the flour sack, he instantly started patting his jacket and pants, digging his hands into his pockets in a flat panic. My bicycle key—where is it? Oh, God, I didn't even lock my bicycle! I left it unlocked outside the grain shop. My bicycle!

And he rushed off toward the grain shop, dehydrated, distraught, heart pounding. In the gathering shadows, nothing felt real: the street seemed to shudder beneath his feet, the darkening sky seemed as if it was crashing around his ears. Nothing felt real—except for the lost money and the bicycle.

TEN

At last, he spotted his bicycle standing against the wall, untouched, unharmed. His burning heart sped, his throat constricted with a mad joy. I could have lost you! For heaven's sake, I could have lost you! he cried out apologetically as he saw the key trailing from the keyhole. Why, that bicycle's worth far more than ten yuan. It could easily have been stolen. I can't believe how stupid I was! Well . . . wait . . . how could someone steal my money and miss my unlocked bicycle? It's not even possible, is it? But then, everything is so unreal!

The heavy wooden door of the grain shop was locked by two fist-sized iron padlocks. The hasps had rusted but the padlocks were new and shining. Two locks for double security. He had himself installed many locks on doors, windows, and furniture, and he knew that all locks could be picked: locks were where locksmiths and thieves converged. As he touched the top padlock a chill ran through him, followed by a rush of fear.

The steps to the grain shop were steep, more than a meter above the ground. He sat on the top step, slouched against the door, feeling as if his body was floating. Still sweating, light-headed from his run, his dampened undershirt slicked against his skin, he raised his sleeve, wiped the sweat off his forehead, and shivered.

Then he lit a cigarette, taking a long slow pull. The smoke eddied and twisted in the dry air like silver-white water vapor, like a memory. How he yearned for a shot of liquor!— for anything that would release the vice around his head.

Closing his eyes, he replayed each moment of the day like the line of a slideshow, ordinary yet subtly monstrous— every moment, every person, every word, every idea, every thought. The timeline remained obdurate: it was only he who shuttled back and forth across it. Then, as he opened his eyes, the smoke cleared, and the line disappeared.

Today has to go on, even if I don't want to, he said to himself: it's not done yet. He took several more pulls, making the cigarette glow, its vapor trickling away. He noticed a fine blue arch amid the wisps of the smoke. *As if time itself was bent.*

Facing the wall of the grain shop, he turned and peed. Passersby, hurrying, paid no attention. *I could pee in the middle of the road, no one would care.*

He sat down, feeling an itch on his back. Reaching beneath his damp undershirt, he scratched it. Yet the itch slowly spread, as if caterpillars were crawling across his back. He checked for insects on the concrete steps, but it was the wrong time of year, of course. As he looked up, the two iron padlocks pierced him like a pair of wicked eyes.

Suddenly he recalled the black cat. Damn it, the cat was probably watching him from behind these very doors! He thought, *That cat must have seen me sitting here all alone. He knows everything. He probably knows where the money is. If the money was stolen, he probably witnessed it!* Thoroughly convinced by this vision, he began to thump on the door with both hands.

Kitty! Meow . . . meow! he called, aping a cat.

The cat's probably resting on the gunnysacks. But when he hears my voice, he'll soon be here! He has a secret to tell. He knows where my money is. He understands how important it is for me to find it . . .

He kept battering at the door, meowing.

Meow . . . meow . . . meow . . . At last, the sound came along from behind the doors. He's coming, he exclaimed, he's coming! He's coming to me!

Overjoyed, he went down on his knees, peeping through the gap between the warped doors. He could see nothing but darkness as deep as a ravine. Through it, he convinced himself that he spotted the cat, pacing in the dark, its unblinking eyes wide. The timing of its pacing was as cool and distant as if the creature was treading in air, soft paws padding invisibly behind the door. Wildly, he stuck his mouth to the gap. The odor of bitter and rotting wood tickled his nose.

Hey! My friend! Hey! Hey! Friend! Can you hear me? Remember me? I was here, just a few hours ago, remember? I lost my money. It's ten yuan, one bill! One single bill! Our food money for this month—food for all five of us. I know you saw something. You were watching. Something happened—I don't know—I'm not sure what—but you know. Tell me, please, say something! Say something to me, I beg! That—that ten yuan note—it's not for luxuries, it's for food! I have a family, you know: I can't afford to lose ten yuan. Food for five! A single note! I lost it here, here in this shop. I looked on the street but I couldn't find it. Did you see what happened? The way your eyes . . . You must know something! And then, and then, I can't go home without it. What could I tell my wife? I beg you! Just say something, please!

With the tip of his nose rubbing against the double doors, he sniffed like a dog. A rush of odor—a dusty, fishy, rat-like odor—penetrated the gap. He believed that the cat was walking toward him, believed he even heard the humming sound of the cat; even believed that the cat was thinking, considering, hesitating about what to do.

His excitement escalated. I know you can hear me. I know you're standing right there, behind these doors! Please talk to me! Please! I can see you. I can smell you! You've just had fish. I can smell it! Hahaha, rats for dinner, right? I can certainly smell the rats! As soon as I walked into this shop . . . To tell you the truth, I can smell a lot of things. I can smell money too—that mucky sweetish smell, but only on payday, haha! Please, come talk to me! Please come closer! I know that you see everything. You can trust me. I'm all alone here! Only me! Only me! My lips are sealed. I talk to no one, not even to my wife. So, no worries, you can trust me. Did you see what happened to my money? Did you see someone steal it? Did you notice? Did you see? Please say something, anything! He was down on all fours, whispering through the doors, entreating, joking, panting.

Then he thought, *Probably he's overeaten and only wishes to sleep.*

So he added: I know that you cats are miraculous, supernatural! With nine lives, right? Right? My mother told me that my grandmother's cat lived for thirty-five years. Thirty-five! Haha! For a cat, that's a damn long life. That cat lived longer than my grandmother. Can you believe that? But you know everything and see everything. Believe me! I know!

A quiet, firm purring emerged from behind the double doors and—this time—the purring was real. Exhilarated, he leaped up. His forehead smashed into the lower padlock, but he was too jubilant to feel the pain. You can hear me, he cried, kneeling down again. I know you're there. I know you can hear me! He squeezed his forefinger into the gap between the doors, but the gap was too narrow. He tried harder and harder until it was injured, jammed.

Can't you see my finger! I'm here, for real. And so, and so

. . . Tell me what you saw this afternoon. Who stole my ten yuan? Ten yuan means a lot to us. Help me to get it back. Help me, please!

But there was no more purring. Eventually, he released his forefinger, bloodied, half-skinned. He straightened up and rocked back on his heels. Then—at a thought—he was down on all fours again. I must sound stupid to you. Do I?! Haha! You don't speak as we speak, but I'm sure you can understand. And you're clever, you can find a way to tell me! Please, I invite you! Come into my dream and tell me what happened. Slide in my dream tonight and confide your message to me. I'll go home and get to sleep right away. I'll wait for you, in my dream. Is that acceptable? I'll wait for you, I promise!

Then he closed his eyes, exhausted. He was thirsty, tired and desperate for sleep. Gradually he slumped on the steps as time went by, patiently waiting for the cat inside to respond. The silence all around—it was mostly silence, the occasional distant crash of crockery or wail from a remote owl seemed loud, painful and real.

He clambered once more to the doors and pressed his ear tightly to the gap. After listening briefly he again started to meow himself—meow, meow—panting the syllables out in an effort to sound more realistic. Once again, that soft response! He imagined that the cat had ambled in the dark toward him and even—stretching, in the way that cats did—scratched the door with its small neat claws: *skrrreeek, skrrreeek, skrrreeek.*

ELEVEN

He followed the moonlight home, carefully negotiating the potholed asphalt, which had been trampled by rutted wheels too long and too often to be repairable. On the rugged surface of the street, the soles of his shoes made crunching noises, as if he was treading on broken bones. He wheeled his bicycle along, rehearsing what to say to his wife.

He thought about lying, yet he could fabricate neither a purpose nor a reason. *I can't do it*, he thought, knowing that one glance from his wife's clear eyes would give the lie to his lie.

Anyway, I lied to the cat already. I told the cat that I'd be going straight home to sleep. That was a lie. I'd rather keep walking until the sun rises. That's how I want to finish today— to wipe it out, as if it had never happened!

Why did I leave the cat? I could easily have slept on the steps of the shop. I don't have to go home to dream! I'll rush back and apologize. Cats are astonishing, miraculous creatures! But I'm almost home. The moonlight's too bright tonight, cruel too.

The courage he had summoned before abandoned him.

His blood chilled when he recalled his wife and children. Yet he kept walking home all the same.

He slowed as he entered the yard. The lights from his neighbors' home glanced off the windows, altering the squares into oblique geometric shapes on the ground, broken, illusory. The contorted shadows disturbed him. The earth shifted and expanded in its own way, yet he seemed to feel the shadows quaking under his thin shoes. What day was it? Tuesday? Thursday? In either case, it was almost over.

He quietly parked his bicycle under the window, slipping under the shadows of the wall, and peered into the room through the glass. His elder daughter sat on a small bench, washing dishes in a big aluminum pot, while his son and younger daughter played chess on the dining table. Sitting on the stool in front of the bed, his wife was still sewing the green silk quilt, her face ashen and drawn. From time to time she glanced up at the window, shook her head and continued sewing.

He knew that she couldn't see him, yet he still felt that their eyes had met, a recognition from the cores of their beings. Her eyes shifted into dark exhaustion as she turned away.

Everything in the room looked just the same. It would probably look the same tomorrow, and in a month, or even in a year's time. The night—like a transparent screen—blocked him, and him alone, outside in the cavernous darkness. He gazed into the shadows on the window, casting about in his mind for ideas of what tomorrow might bring.

Tonight, he lacked the courage to even open the door.

He trudged to the shack, switched on the light, tossed the empty flour sack onto the bedside table, and collapsed on the bed.

How tired he was!

Three years ago, he'd built the shack—himself—from scratch. For six months he had spent every evening and most Sundays wheeling the building materials in a small handcart, assembling brick walls, installing windows and doors, constructing the wooden sheathing roof and overlaying it with tarred paper—not to mention finishing the concrete floor, painting the walls, and carpentering beds and tables for his children. He worked logically, like a born engineer, finishing everything to perfection. His children, who were growing fast, needed space for themselves. They were thrilled when they first moved in. But once winter came, everything changed.

In the winter, lacking a stove, the shack was no better than an ice cellar, only useful for storing cabbage and firewood. The glass window and door were covered with layers of wrinkled white ice, which refused to melt until spring.

Baba, why can't we have a stove in our room? His elder daughter once asked at the dinner table, looking straight into his eyes.

We can't afford enough coal and firewood for two stoves,

his wife had intervened, plastering an awkward smile on her face. Anyway, it's nice to share one room in winter. It's cozy and convenient.

Just stop, will you? I'm asking Baba, not you. Can't afford this, can't afford that—is there anything we *can* afford? You should've thought about the coal, the firewood, and the stupid winter when you first built the stupid room! And really, what was the point of building it if we can't afford a stove? The shack's just a piece of useless ice-shit now, with all five of us packed ass-to-ass in this shitty room for the whole winter! How can you say it's convenient? How can you feel that it's cozy? Do *you* feel it's cozy?—I certainly don't. There isn't even room enough to fart! Then the girl had given everyone in the room the evil eye.

Her acid adolescent fury had roiled the room: not even his wife had been able to hold her gaze. *Sometimes he thought that his elder daughter was some kind of vicious animal, jeering, sneering, hyena-like . . .*

Baba, answer me! I want to stay in my room. What's wrong with that? You could just install a stove, couldn't you?

He'd chomped on his food, his face dull and heavy. Not saying a word.

Be quiet, will you? We're all enjoying our dinner! His wife had shushed her.

Then they'd started exchanging words. Caught in the crossfire, he hadn't dared to look at either of them. But he had still been able to sense their eyes firing at each other, eyes burning with anger and scorched with distress. Finally, his daughter had tossed her chopsticks on the table, stood up and stormed out, not returning home until late in the evening.

After this, she'd hardly talked to him for the rest of the winter. This cold-shouldering drama then endured for three consecutive winters. He bore his daughter no grudge for it. He had even secretly apologized to her, more than once. *Listen, I've done my best. Perhaps I'm just one of those men who cannot keep his promises.* It made it even worse when he recalled his father and his own childhood, remembering how he'd sworn never to let his children suffer. Well, they were suffering now.

Where have you been? The door was flung open and his wife stood accusingly in the doorway, her tone expressing all the frustration and worry that she had suffered. He almost jumped.

Where in heaven's name—she suddenly paused, mid-sentence, shocked at his broken condition. His eyelashes were fluttering nervously, his hands clenched together, raw blood stained his fingers. His hair was smutted with debris; and the inch-long cut on his forehead above his right eyebrow was blotted with dried blood. He was smeared with dust and sweat, his clothes were bedraggled and covered with dirt, and two buttons on his jacket were missing. He looked as if he had fallen into a drainage ditch and crawled home.

What happened? What's wrong? Tell me!

As he gulped, she shook his shoulders. Just tell me, tell me! What happened? Tell me what happened!

He mumbled: I lost the money for the flour. I lost ten yuan. I lost it.

She had to lean closer to hear. To her, he seemed to have aged two decades in just a few hours. Her pretty ears looked soft and pink, almost translucent, hovering before him. He shifted his eyes across her face, from ear to ear, from cheek to cheek. Anything to avoid her eyes.

Lost? How? Eh? How did you lose it? Tell me. Tell me!

In her distress, she squeezed his shoulders harder, her face twisting. He ached under her hands. She seemed even more panicked than he!

How? Eh? Tell me! Tell me! Don't just stand here, say something!

She almost choked, digging her hands harder and deeper into his skin.

I—I just—I just lost it! I got to the grain shop, I waited in the queue, of course, and then it was gone! The money was gone! He delved into his pockets, taking out the two yuan and seventy-five cents, the ration card, the cigarette pack, and the matchbox, and set them on the edge of the bed.

These are all I have. It's lost. It's lost—it's lost! He began to whimper, licking his dry cracked lips. He looked as helpless as a young boy who had misbehaved and awaited his punishment.

A premonition of dread flickered through her. She could only motion for him to sit on the bed, and mechanically pat his shoulder. She could manage no more, in terms of consolation. Weak and shaky, she would have preferred to lean her shoulder against his—but she didn't dare, in case he crumpled altogether. He was blinking desperately, trying to hold back his tears. She had never seen him weep before, not even at his mother's funeral.

The space in the room seemed suddenly empty, filled with air too thin for them to breathe. There were only the two of them, but the silence distanced them from each other.

She longed to hold him in her arms, to say: It's all right. If it's lost, it's lost—so be it. Don't feel so bad. But she could not, numbed as she was by fear, she could not console him now. She felt ashamed of her mercilessness, yet she could not help it. She kept thinking, *We can't afford to lose ten yuan. That's one month's worth of food for our entire family!* But this man had lost it, the money that they had been waiting for so long.

Lit by sudden anger, she longed for the relief of blaming and scolding him. Yet she did not dare. She just stood, entirely helpless. *I can't bear this*, she thought and moved to the door.

I must return to the children, she said. You stay here. Her voice sounded so remote that not even she fully heard it.

Swallowing all her comforting words—but swallowing all the bile and blame too—she left the room.

TWELVE

He lay down, still fully clothed, facing the wall. As soon as he closed his eyes, that straight line jumped before him, glittering. Lao Qi, Xiao Yang, the pregnant doctor, Xiao Ma, Accountant Liu, the chairman of the Labor Union, the fat woman in the grain shop and the male clerk all stood before him, absurd expressions on their faces. The cat was there too, on the gunnysacks, alert and watchful. He could smell a bizarre mix of machine oil, money, medicine, grain, rat droppings. They were blended—the odors of dream and reality—but which was which? Drifting off, he spoke aloud, half-dreaming: I told you I would dream. I didn't lie! Talk to me, please! I know you were watching. I know you saw what had happened. I know you saw everything. I can see you through the wall.

His hands reached out, stroking the wall, and then meticulously began to scratch it, skrrreeek, skrrreeek, skrrreeek . . .

It was almost midnight when his wife returned with a mug of water and his blood pressure pills. Putting them on the bedside table, she asked if he wanted something to eat. Still

facing the wall, he waved her away. She was more than a little shocked to notice the streaks of fresh-peeled paint from
off the wall. Instead of mentioning it, she covered him gently
with a quilt, patted him on his leg, turned off the light and
left him.

The instant she left, he sat up, listening to the muffled
whispers—a man and a woman—through the wall. He could
not discern the words, but the tones sounded strange, and the
ticking of their clock rang eerily in his ears. He listened until
the whispers were replaced with the sound of water, probably
being poured from a kettle to a basin. Then more muffled dis-
cussion, soft water, dry coughs, a long, relieved sigh.

Moonlight shone through the glass, casting irregular
shapes on wall and floor. The room he had laboriously built
from scratch became barren and unrecognizable, submerged
into the shallow vacancy of the unknowable.

Outside, there was the distant creak of a door. Lao
Song, two doors away, trudged into his yard, coughed
and spat loudly.

It's past midnight already. Why is he up so late? Latrine?
He listened intently as Lao Song wandered through the yard,
until the sound of his ambling footsteps echoed away.

Feeling the sores on his fingers, he lifted his hands to his
nose, smelling the plaster from the wall, and remembered—
with a pang—the black cat.

I slept, but the cat refused to come to my dream. Perhaps

the money wasn't stolen, after all? Or perhaps it slipped down a pothole. Lao Song might even have found it and pocketed it.

He dangled his legs over the edge of the bed, searching for his shoes with his toes. He thought about following Lao Song to the latrine, then changed his mind.

I'm not a lunatic and I don't want him to think that I might be. Also, I'd need a flashlight and I don't have one. Not one with a working battery, at any rate.

Although he couldn't help picturing Lao Song finding the ten yuan note on the street, that fat smug grin spreading over his face. Suddenly he felt scalded with anger. *You rat! That's my money. It's mine. You rat! You rat!* Feeling his way toward the window, he stood on tiptoe, resting his chin on the windowsill, waiting for his anger to seep away as the chill from the concrete floor crept into his feet.

The window was high, as he'd built a shed underneath it to store coal; the roof was covered with tarred paper to keep out the rain. Moonlight cast a layer of silver organza on the tar, making it shimmer and wave, like ripples on the surface of water. He could see the rooms opposite in the darkness against the starlit sky, yet nothing moved but those shallow shimmering ripples. He somehow felt that he was drifting in a boat on a still river.

Flat footsteps approached. Lao Song, carrying something round (perhaps a spittoon?) The creak of a door followed, then stillness was restored.

With pins and needles in his legs, he staggered back to bed and curled up under the quilt.

But what am I going to do when morning comes? I still need to buy flour. We all need to eat. And what about the money? It's lost! It's lost!

He drew back in dismay at the thought of dawn. Suddenly he thought: *My sister!—she's my only hope. She's always been my savior. She trusts me; she gave me a key to her flat, years ago. She knows that I would never lie. She'll understand, she always does! I lost the money—though—I don't know—it might have been stolen—but I could never have a better excuse to borrow more.*

He turned down the quilt and stretched his legs, tingling with relief.

How stupid I've been! I should have gone to her the moment I left the grain shop. I must have lost my wits yesterday! It's too late to go now, of course. I simply need to borrow another ten yuan from her. No, wait—ten yuan wouldn't be enough to survive the whole month. Perhaps twenty. That's it! Twenty yuan will do, because my wife will be able to make extra from babysitting.

Anxiety swept over him. Never had he been so eager to see his sister. He sat upright, groping desperately for his matchbox, his cigarettes. After a few pulls, his tension abated, and his excitement too: *What an idiot you are! She might agree to loan you the money, but that would only add to my cur-*

rent debt, ninety yuan will become one hundred and ten. It's too much debt for me to ever repay! But then, think of all the chores I've done for her, day after day, month after month, year after year!

Then his sister's acid tones sneered inside his head. (Oh, don't get me wrong. I know how hard it must be for five of you to exist on your own salary. I don't even mind loaning you money—as long as I have any, that is. But really, you could try a little harder! Pay a visit to the homes of your general manager or the Chairman of the Labor Union, taking a nice gift! Go to the Community Committee in Worker Village and ask them to find your wife a job! Just do *something!*)

That *something* was the most frustrating of all.

His last pull on his cigarette end burned the tip of his finger, yet he felt no pain, thinking: *Anyway, today is finished. It's been wiped out somehow. If only my life could come to a standstill here, then everything would be fine.*

He hesitated, remembering all the things that he'd promised to do for others: mending the water bucket for Grandma Chen—he might manage it tomorrow?—painting the walls of his sister's home, replacing the broken mirror of her armoire, repairing the roof for the Yangs, installing fluorescent lights for Xiao Ma, making a kitchen window for Lao Qi . . .

They could just get by without him.

Lying down, his fingers stroked curves across the wall, pausing, and then stroking again, as if he was inscribing calligraphy but had forgotten the characters. Gradually the coolness of the wall pulsed through his fingers.

He was thinking about his sister's flat: the furniture, her windows and doors, even the smell of her home. He took a tour of her rooms in his mind, pacing through the rooms, step by step.

His mind brimmed: the walls, the armoire, the chiffonier, the cupboard, the beds, the desk, the trunks, the washstand, dining tables, chairs and stools, the two winter stoves. He had installed the stoves as well as all the lights: he was as familiar with those two rooms as he was with his own home. He had repaired and repainted the furniture, fixed the table lamp, replaced the mirrors, changed the doorknobs, installed the mortice lock on the entry door . . .

The mortice lock. Suddenly the mortice lock on the door and the key on his keyring sprang up like tiny bells, hovering, tinkling. Dangerously alert, he thought harder. *The key. The lock.*

The LOCK! A flash like an electric shock—with afterburn—streaked through him. Out of nowhere, he was possessed by something chilling, terrifying. His heart bounded, his face hardened, his body stiffened. The air seemed suddenly heavier. The room, the bed—even the concrete floor—almost seemed to give way beneath him.

His sister had once asked him to install a lock to her desk. (As she had put it: I have nothing to hide, exactly. But I have things that I can't afford to lose, like the residence permit, coupons, ration cards—functional things, things that we can't live without. We're never home during the day, but Lulu runs in and out, sometimes she even brings her friends here. And you know what the children here are like! I wouldn't trust them farther than I could throw them! *That's* why I need a lock on the drawer, just to be on the safe side.)

He had installed a match-box-sized iron padlock in under ten minutes. And, every time he borrowed money, his sister would go into the backroom, unlock the drawer of the desk . . .

But locks can be unlocked—locks can even be picked.

The thought snaked through his body like a bolt of lightning. He felt shaken, disturbed, vividly, even horrifyingly alive. He strained against the darkness until his eyes ached, as if trying to blink away the craziness from inside his head. He leaned his hot face against the wall, cooling it a little.

Despite his shock, the thoughts running through his mind were calm and coherent, and pointed to one conclusion—a way to "wipe out" yesterday and to move on. Vague feelings of nerves and uncertainty gradually crystallized into something far more confident.

Damn! I can do it! I know I can do it! he thought.

He lay back down and forced himself to breathe.

He had no notion what time it was, yet the moonlight still edged into invisible blackness. His gaze, roaming restless over the room, saw nothing but the silhouette of the small blurred window, on which he suddenly observed two tiny suggestions of gleaming brightness, wavering back and forth.

Like the eyes of a cat.

THIRTEEN

He fell asleep around dawn, dreamlessly. Neighbors talked, coughed and spat, doors opened and closed, water was poured and splashed, firewood was chopped and stoves were lit—but this had long been the morning chorus of his life. He slept so deeply that he awoke completely tranquil, as if the previous day's trauma had left no trace at all.

Looking out of the window, he realized he had overslept and felt reality seeping into his body again. Slowly, he recollected the previous day, attempting to fill the gaps in his memory. He heard his elder daughter emerge, utter something in an unpleasant tone, slam the door, and leave. *She never was a morning person.*

When his wife knocked on the door, he closed his eyes and didn't even stir.

We're going to the dairy for the milk, she told him. Behind her, he discerned the soft flute-like chattering of his son and younger daughter. Eventually, all their footsteps faded away.

He instantly sat up and donned his shoes, lighting a cigarette, and looking with distaste at the creases in the trousers

in which he had slept. For a while he paced, finishing his cigarette and clearing his head.

Then he walked into the room across the yard, washed his
face and brushed his teeth. He stood in front of the mirror,
pulling his hair down slightly to cover the cut on his forehead, then studied his face for a minute: he didn't look too
bad. The room was spotless, with a fresh-made bed, dusted
furniture and cleaned floor. And his wife had even packed
his lunch box and left it on the dining table, *as if it was just
another day*. He chose a clean jacket, then picked up his black
bag and walked back to the shack.

He pulled the toolbox from under the bed, selected a small
hammer and a screwdriver, and added them to his grain ration card and flour sack in the bag, along with a pair of old
cotton gloves. He fingered the keychains, repeatedly check-
ing that he had everything he needed. Finally, he locked the
doors, hung the bag on the handlebars of his bicycle and ped-
dled off.

The streets seemed strangely empty. Less than ten minutes
later, he found himself already outside his sister's flat. Glancing around cautiously, he failed to see any familiar faces,
though two housewives with baskets were turning into the
alleyway, gossiping hard.

He wheeled his bicycle into the entrance and parked it
under the stairway. *Don't lock it. You'll be right back*, he reminded himself. Then he removed the gloves from the bag

and slipped them on. Gloved, bag in hand, he walked lightly up the stairs.

It was an old, Soviet-style, four-story building. Two stairs up led to the first-floor landing, where a concrete trough for tap water faced the stairs. There were toilets on either side, one for men and one for women, and two homes on either side of the toilets. His sister's was on the right.

In the dingy light on the landing, it was next to impossible to see anything other than the outlines of greenish doors leading to each flat. From the left-hand side came the crackly sound of a male newscaster broadcasting the editorial of *The People's Daily*. The woman who lived there—paralyzed in a work injury—almost never left home.

He stood on the landing for a moment, warily listening for any sound besides the blaring radio—though assuming that everyone would be out at this hour, whether at school or at work. Then he walked silently to the door of his sister's flat, and soundlessly unlocked the door.

He slipped into the room and gently closed the door behind him. The two rooms were only separated by a wooden door frame with a cloth curtain, patterned with faded palm leaves, and permeated by the reek of stale leftovers. He took a hasty look around the first room, remembering that the mirror on the armoire was broken, and that he'd been asked—by his brother-in-law—to replace it.

Noticing the splashed tea stains on the wall, he smiled ruefully. *My sister has always had a temper.* He checked the window, selecting the piece of glass he would purposely break after he'd finished.

He lifted the curtain and went into the back room. There, he set down his bag, retrieved his hammer and screwdriver, prized the hasp from the lock and forced the drawer open—all in a matter of minutes. He was greeted by a pile of documents—residence permit, grain ration card, marriage certificate—neatly stacked in the corner. A bulging paper bag contained a half-bag of Cuban brown sugar. A red armband stenciled with the characters *East is Red* was folded into a small package. When he unwrapped it, a brand-new Shanghai woman's watch fell onto his hand. (He had never seen his sister wearing a watch.) He rewrapped the watch in its original packaging and replaced it. He had no use for a watch. It was valuable—but exchanging it for cash would cause nothing but trouble.

He rapidly flicked through a pile of envelopes, finding nothing but old letters. Three brown envelopes that lay at the very end of the drawer proved more fruitful: a stack of coupons for cloth, some food ration stamps worth twenty-five kilos of grain, and thirty-five yuan, in notes. He swiftly pocketed the food ration stamps and the thirty-five yuan and shut the drawer.

Hurry up, leave! he urged himself, as he bent down to

gather his tools. Then, from just behind him, came a fragile, frightened voice: Jiu Jiu?

That simple syllable was powerful enough to destroy him. He flinched as if struck and then froze, attempting to collect his lost wits.

Jiu Jiu! *You?* That sweet, girlish voice echoed around the room, pounding against his ears. He turned swiftly, plastering on a broad, faked smile. Lulu stood in the door frame, her key in her left hand and the cloth curtain in her right, the green leaves of its pattern caressing that pretty, frowning face.

Ah, ah, Lulu, he faltered. Lulu, I'm j-just getting something—something f-for your mother!

The silence was horrible.

His young niece's eyes, brimming with shock and suspicion, pierced him to the bone. His stammering seemed to shriek aloud of guilt.

Pull yourself together, moron. She's only a child!

Your father had an accident at work, he said, more quietly. I—ah—I came to get some money, as your mother asked.

Accident?! What kind of accident? Is he all right? She whipped back, shuddering at the thought.

I don't know. I'm just going back to the hospital now, he said, starting to gather up his tools.

Baba is in *hospital*? she howled, almost weeping.

Yes, yes, I'm heading back there, he said, feigning a worry which affected her instantly.

But—but then, it must be serious! In hospital! Actually in the hospital? What's happened to him? What? Then, staring at her uncle's face, his gloved hands, the tools scattered on the floor and the pried-open hasp, her previous suspicions returned, thinking: *I thought Baba is out of town?!*

He couldn't meet her flaming eyes. All he could do was to say, as quietly as he could: I'm unsure of the details. Your mother called me at the factory and sent me here to get the money.

And, his mind made up, he bagged everything swiftly.

I'm going to the hospital now, he said. Do you want to come with me?

Yes, all right, Lulu muttered, secretly unconvinced.

Come then, let's go together, he said, setting his teeth on the last word. And there, in the doorway, one step away from her, he dropped his bag and, with a fierce stretch of muscle, seized her by the throat. The flesh that he clutched between his fingers was warm and soft. *Such a small throat. Like a kitten's.* His hands twisted even harder.

Jiu . . .

Lulu gave a low choking moan and began to tremble violently. He stood, as steadfast as if hammered into the earth. Nothing could shatter him now. Pinned against the doorframe, unleashing blind and useless kicks, Lulu latched on to the curtain with her right hand, desperate to keep her foothold. The curtain swayed wildly between them: again, he smelled the stale grease. The moment seemed endless, but finally, finally, the curtain gave way. Slumping backward, she slid to the floor, with an empurpled face and wide-opened eyes, still clutching her key in her left hand and the curtain in her right.

His mind went blank for a moment as he looked at her. Then he dragged the curtain down, in a single movement, and fiercely wrapped it around her neck and head, his hands trembling, his head whirling. He tried to reassure himself, saying aloud: *You did well, no blood, no mess. You did well.*

It sounded false, even to himself. He wiped the cold sweat off his forehead. Then he noticed the key in Lulu's hand, a key attached to a small dragonfly pendant with red plastic string. He forced her fisted fingers open and removed it, rubbing its surface with his gloves and carefully placing it on top of the cupboard where it was normally kept. On the lower shelf, he noticed the cookie tin that his brother-in-law had bought at the bakery the previous day. He opened the lid: there were still five cookies left. He picked one up with his middle and index finger, popped it into his mouth and put the lid back on, wiping a few crumbs off the shelf.

Suddenly, miraculously, his mind felt perfectly organized and sharp. He walked to the entrance and locked the door. Then he retrieved a soiled gunnysack and some hemp twine from the cupboard, and strode to the back room, standing for a moment in front of his sister's bed, piled up with pillows, quilts and sheets. He selected a sheet from the pile and laid it on the floor.

Then he dragged Lulu's body to one side of the sheet and rolled it up as tightly as he could. He crimped the edge of the sheet roll, bagged it securely inside the gunnysack, and bound it up tightly with twine.

Hurry! Hurry! he thought, but he remained agile and calm, swift and absorbed, like an infantryman packing his combat load, counting the minutes in his mind, knowing that he couldn't waste even a second.

Finally, he stood up and checked both rooms meticulously. Everything appeared exactly as it had when he had arrived—other than Lulu's key on the cupboard. He had originally planned to break the glass with a hammer and to unbolt the window—suggesting a common burglary—but this would no longer be required.

Clamping the gunnysack under his right arm—its weight rather astonished him—he maneuvered toward the front door, the black bag in his left hand.

There, he turned back and glanced around one last time. Suddenly he staggered in horror, dropping the gunnysack heavily to the floor.

A black cat sat on the window ledge, its face so flattened against the glass that it appeared almost deformed. Its eyes were suffused with vigilance—with brute animal instinct.

The cat from the grain shop! He almost shouted it. His

throat burned, as if he'd swallowed a piece of blazing hot tofu too late to spit it out. Trying to compose himself, he looked again, and felt a little reassured. *No, no, this must be a wild cat—this cat had green eyes, not the yellowish-amber of the cat from the grain shop.*

The cat twitched its tail, eyes blazing, and began to scratch the glass: *skrrreeek, skrrreeek, skrrreeek* . . . That sound, for a moment, almost unmanned him. But then he reasoned: *Even if it is the same animal, well, so what? Cats can't talk! Get moving! Hurry! Leave, leave!*

He grasped the gunnysack again and unlocked the door, pausing to check for any noises from the landing. It seemed exactly as before: the newscaster was still loudly broadcasting from the opposite apartment. As he stepped from the room, he imagined he heard the cat hiss from behind him.

Through the glass? Impossible!

He gently closed the door, moved soundlessly along the landing and slipped down the stairs. Beneath his bicycle seat, he retrieved the hemp rope. He then bound the gunnysack skillfully—though with some difficulty—to the back seat. As he hung the black bag on the handlebar, he paused, afraid he'd forgotten something. Then he wheeled the bicycle out of the building, a look of calm plastered to his face, and cycled away.

FOURTEEN

As he rode through the early spring breeze, feeling the unaccustomed heaviness—the lack of balance—from his burden, his thoughts turned to the small river that ran behind Worker Village. He had a strange instinct that somewhere along the river was the place he needed to make today disappear. He had managed to expunge yesterday—and he was doing his utmost to wipe out today. He was possessed by a chaotic, fervent idea that, after these aberrations, he would be able to move on and busy himself helping others. He imagined himself repairing his sister's mirror, salvaging Grandma Chen's water-bucket . . .

Still, he retained some sense of caution. Instead of turning left toward the river, he circled around in the opposite direction, in hopes of missing passing neighbors or acquaintances. As he crossed through a small alley, he suddenly recalled his sister's tale of a local schoolgirl being raped and gave his upper lip a nervous touch.

At least I don't have a mustache . . .

The narrow river that ran behind Worker Village had

long since become less a river than a stagnant backwater. Its riverbed was clogged with sewage, sludge and rubbish that locals had abandoned: rotting vegetables, tree leaves, scraps of paper and debris floated on its filthy water. People littered cinder and firewood ash, household mess—even excrement—on both sides, turning the riverbank into little more than a convenient dump.

A few local families who had lost babies had dug pits and buried the corpses on the slopes of the river. They often tied a small stripe of white cloth to a stick, with the baby's name on the cloth, as markers for future visits. But these sticks were often tossed away, lost or simply swamped with trash.

A few years before, he'd been passing by the river on his way home when he noticed a woman burning paper[5] in the dark. Waving her cigarette passionately, she'd cried out: I cannot find you, dear one—I'm so sorry, but somehow, I lost you! Some bastard took away your stick: these people have no hearts! But it's really my own fault, I'm so useless, too useless even to keep watch over a single stick! I will never find you again! I know you feel lonely down there—I know I should have come to see you more often—but I couldn't—I can't—I have to work—I have to take care of your sisters—not to mention that damn drunk! But I have never forgotten about you.

---

5 Burning paper is a mourning tradition in China, as ceremonial offerings to the departed.

How could I? Never, never! I miss you every day! Please, for-give me! I'm so sorry, so sorry, so very, very sorry . . .

There the woman had squatted, wiping her tears and her nose on her sleeve, utterly oblivious of everyone and every-thing beyond the intensity of her grief.

He might have paid no attention—for he'd been accus-tomed to such scenes on the riverbank. Yet this woman had been peculiar—charismatic, neurotic—and her words had somehow caught him by surprise. She had talked in great rolling phrases and in a powerful voice, as if to ensure that her apology would be heard.

He'd gone on his way feeling blessed, as his wife had al-ready given birth to three thriving, healthy babies. That night, as he held his wife's soft body against his, he found himself carried away by the fire of ardent desire stirred deep within him. And afterwards, as they lay silently in each other's arms, his wife had run her fingers gently along the curves of his chest, whispering into his ear: It's been a long time since . . .

Her tone had been sweet yet distant. There was always something he didn't entirely understand. But he generally pretended to agree, to please her.

Yes, too long, he'd said, shifting sideways, afraid that she could feel the quivering of his heart. A sudden chill, like a current, had passed through him.

We forget so many things, she had murmured.

Like what?

Like what we did when we were young.

Yes, he'd agreed, still unsure of what she meant, and suddenly recalling the woman at the riverbank. *Would she forget about her baby one day? Or never?*

The kids are growing, she'd reminded him, her fingers sliding lightly over his bare belly.

Yes—breathing in the sweetness from her breath, feeling more grateful than ever to the mother of his children. How strong she was!

It will get better, he'd added, drawing her closer, to reassure her—or perhaps himself.

He remembered that night just as he reached the winding path along the river, heading west.

The city limit was perhaps fifty minutes' ride away. There, he knew, there was a chemical plant, an abandoned bridge, and—beyond that—boundless stretches of cropland. He sometimes visited a village in the area, one studded with low, broken-down farmhouses. For the past few months, if unable to buy eggs at the black market, he would cycle there after dark, to purchase eggs from the farmers. He was as familiar with the route as if it had been drawn on paper.

He stayed on the road, trying to appear as unhurried and inconspicuous as possible, only speeding up when passing pedestrians or other cyclists. Several honey wagons and garbage carts passed him, drawn by horses or donkeys. The farmers, all in tattered clothes and straw hats, seemed to hold their whips lax in their hands, almost nodding off. Some came almost head-on toward him, only swerving at the last moment.

Two tractors loaded with battered farm tools flashed past in the opposite direction, blowing cinder motes and grit into his face. He coughed and rubbed his eyes with his sleeve but kept going.

From behind, he heard the rattling chatter of two young male cyclists, probably workers at the chemical plant. He deliberately allowed them to overtake him, then trailed behind, keeping a discreet distance. Eventually, they turned off at a crossroad and disappeared.

The land on the other side of the river was mostly comprised of new-plowed fields, beyond which he could see neither houses nor people. The forbidding metal smokestacks of the chemical plant towered above, its exhaust fumes—steaming through its chimneys and puffing incessantly into the sky—seemed to take the edge off the sun's own brightness. Its steep wall, festooned with prison-styled barbed wire, loomed over him. Wild-grown weeds and wilted thick bushes clustered along the wall where, at night, the homeless sometimes sheltered—just then, he couldn't see a soul. He hastened his pace, occasionally choking, on harsh chemicals from one side or overpowering manure on the other.

Once he'd passed the chemical plant, a half-collapsed bridge skewed into view, its dank riverbanks covered with garbage and rubble. Withered trees leaned against the road-side, a few marcescent leaves on their branches.

He stopped and parked his bicycle under a tree bent aslant in the winds. There he squatted down, lit a cigarette—and waited. He waited until there was nothing and no one to be seen or heard. Then he rose and swiftly unloaded the gun-nysack from the back seat. Clamping it hard under his arm, cigarette still in his mouth, he half-walked, half-trotted down the slope. Halfway toward the water, he stopped, breathing fast, and put down the sack. Then, with a single fluid move-ment he kicked it—hard. The sack stuttered and then started to roll, skidding down toward the river faster than he had expected. At one point it hit a ridge and paused—his heart momentarily stopped. Then it resumed its inexorable roll to-ward the river.

There wasn't much splash. The sack started to sink almost immediately, releasing shallow silver circles on the greenish water. For a second he felt that he might have seen those rip-ples somewhere, but had forgotten when and where . . .

He stood, for a moment, oblivious of the passage of time. The breeze blew the ash off his cigarette, layering the front of his jacket. He dusted it off with his hand, unbuttoned his pants, and urinated. He urinated as far and as high as he could, just as he had when showing off, when he'd been very small. Along with two or three friends, he'd used to stand at corners of the school playground, urinating and laughing hysterically—though always careful not to stain his pants. (His mother had beaten him if she found urine stains on his pants.)

He felt sad when he thought about his mother, and sadder still when he noticed his elder daughter taking spiteful pleasure in irritating others. At such times he thought, *It's in our blood*—and could scarcely help feeling superstitious.

Hurry up! Get going! he urged, buttoning up his pants and releasing the last pull of his cigarette. The curled ripples, of a crepuscular green, had gradually slipped away, stirred by the breeze on the sour water.

He stubbed out the cigarette on his shoe and pushed the cigarette end into his pocket. *It's over. Wiped out. Everything is wiped out—yesterday—today—all gone, all finished!* he murmured, as he returned to his bicycle.

FIFTEEN

Suddenly, it had turned much colder—that brittle, wintry feel that he loathed, the air reeking of cooked cabbage. He had perspired so much that his undershirt clung to his skin. *You pussy!* he mocked.

He had to slow down, as he experienced a cramp in his right leg. Still cycling, he wriggled his toes, combatting the soreness—but the cramps only worsened.

In the end he stopped by the curb of the road, kneading his leg. Suddenly he felt stranded in enemy territory. The dirt road wound down continuously, over torturous bumps, through villages and farmland before disappearing into the horizon. Hands gripping the handlebars of his bicycle, he watched the barren countryside, the towering smokestacks of the chemical plant, and the ramshackle farmhouses settling into their backdrop of dark fields and ruined bridges.

For a second he stood motionless, contemplating the bizarreness of simply being there, in the moment, entirely alone—like a stray dog.

Just leave! he commanded.

When had he started talking to himself?

The ride back to the city was exhausting. The cramps shifted from his legs to his stomach; every thrust on the pedals became an exercise of will. But he was so hungry—he had eaten almost nothing for twenty hours! He suddenly recollected a baozi shop near the Children's Hospital, a bistro where he'd taken his son after visiting the hospital the previous autumn.

It had been an important treat: the first time his son had ever been to a bistro. As they walked in, his son, despite his pallor, had glanced at him with a shy smile, trying to rein in his excitement, his face aglow with contentment. At that moment, smiling down at his boy, he could not have felt prouder or happier.

They had shared a table with an older couple. The wife had a deep-furrowed face and held a ragbag tightly to her chest. She'd grumbled nonstop to her husband, his knitted beanie pulled down around his eyebrows.

I don't understand why we have to eat here, wasting our ration stamp and money for some baozi that tastes like shit! We should've gone home and cooked something for ourselves—but you'll never know how tired I feel, always fighting with you!

Then don't, her husband had said, curtly. Quit talking.

I don't want to eat with you.

Then go home.

I won't go home and cook today. You hear me?

Listen, everybody cooks! What's so special about you?

I'm not going to cook today, she said. Understand?

Starve yourself then, why don't you?—lazy-ass! At least the shit here will taste good.

She'd said: I don't know how you'd cope without me.

Oh, I'd cope, don't you worry!

They'd shelved their argument as he and his son had approached their table.

Are you all right? the woman had suddenly asked his son, whose face was puffy, and whose eyelids were swollen.

The boy, daunted by such a sudden question from a stranger, had lowered his gaze, and twisted his small fingers on the table.

Is he your son? The husband had wanted to know.

Yes, he'd told him, slightly annoyed.

Is he all right?

He's okay, he'd said reluctantly. He has acute nephritis.

The boy had shifted his body closer to his father, as if shamed.

The woman had said sharply: If that's the case, you shouldn't bring him here to eat. The food here is too salty. It's not good for him. It's not good for anyone, really.

Suddenly he'd remembered the doctor's warning about cutting salt from his son's diet.

You're right, I completely forgot, he'd told her, and summoned an awkward smile to his lips.

Turning to his son, he noticed how furious he was. It's all

right. Just this once, he'd said, giving the boy a knowing pat on his back.

As their number was called, the couple had stood up and hurried to the counter for their food. The boy's unease had disappeared.

Baba, what's the stuffing here? he'd asked, his little wan face glimmering.

Pork and cabbage.

My mama can make pork and cabbage stuffing too. But it smells so delicious here! The boy had raised his head, wrinkled his nose, and stuck his tongue out for a second, as if the tongue itself could smell.

Well, they have a chef in the kitchen. How can any mother compare with a chef?

Baba, is beef tasty? I mean, does it taste as good as pork? the boy had asked in a lower voice, as the couple were returning to the table. There had been no need to speak to them again, however: eyes glued to their plates, they'd chewed with their mouths full, and paid no attention to anything else.

It's so-so, it has a gamey taste, he'd replied, trying to remember the last time that he'd had beef—before he was married, certainly. The boy had picked up the vinegar cruet on the table, pouring some into his father's plate, then his own.

Our neighbor Wang Lao Lao[6] always makes baozi with

---

6 Lao Lao: maternal grandmother in Chinese. Children also use it for any elderly women, to show respect.

beef stuffing, the boy had confided, as if reporting someone else's secret.

That's because the Wangs are Muslims. They can't eat pork.

What are Muslims?

They're from a different culture. I don't know much about them, except that they abstain from eating pork and dislike the word *pig*. Muslims convert the surname *Zhu*[7] to *Hei*. So if you hear that someone's surname is *Hei*, you'll know they must be Muslims. Muslims buy beef and mutton with special coupons. But because we're Han we can't buy beef or mutton.

Suddenly, he'd remembered the commander, the general manager, and the army ration card that his colleagues so envied—and he'd wished to apologize to his son for not being allowed to procure beef for him to try.

Neither of them ever mentioned the bistro afterwards. The boy, always sensitive to the feelings of others, had kept it secret for fear of jealousy. Yet the little expedition had still brought his son closer to him. After the trip, the boy had started following him around, offering to help when he worked at home, showing great interest in his tools, and helping to tidy his toolbox.

By the time he had cycled to the baozi shop, it was past lunchtime. The smell of food and coal smoke suddenly brought loneliness upon him—he decided he was missing his son.

A homeless man sprawled in the lee of the wall, half-covered

---

7 In Chinese, the character *Zhu* has the same pronunciation as *pig*.

by tattered rags and scraps of cardboard, his blackened feet stuck out. There was a broken mug near his head with a couple of one-cent coins in it. He faced the sun with clasped-shut eyes, his long scruffy hair covering most of his face. *Have mercy on me! Please!* he shouted whenever he sensed a passer-by, adding a sepulchral touch to the atmosphere.

He parked his bicycle and locked it. His fingers fumbled, before emerging with a five-cent coin. He tossed it into the mug without even looking at the tramp.

He ordered six baozi and a large cup of liquor, choosing the seat farthest from two men in their forties, wearing ragged work uniforms and caps. They already seemed at least half-drunk, with burnished faces and raised voices.

As he waited to be served, the rumbling in his stomach intensified: the aroma of food and alcohol tantalized him. The moment he received his cup he instantly gulped it down. The cheap, strong chill rushed through his throat: his stomach felt scorched yet warmed. Gradually, relaxation set in.

He devoured the first two baozi without even tasting them, then, the edge of his hunger blunted, he attempted to use his chopsticks to pick up the third. Suddenly his right hand began to shake and twitch spasmodically. He put the chopsticks down, gently massaging his stiff and aching knuckles. For a moment he stared at his hands—rough, competent, handy— as if he didn't recognize them.

You can fix anything, can't you? He told them, with a strange little laugh.

Before long he was replete and mellow, slightly tipsy. *Now I'm at least a little happier than a starved dog*, he thought, recalling the lost feeling he'd experienced on the road.

Then he lit a cigarette, narrowing his eyes among the wisp of smoke. The straight line from yesterday, on which all the marks of happenings had been inscribed, refused to resurface: his memories of the morning were comprised in a vain gasp for breath and a mocking meow. Time, before his eyes, wavered, decelerated, then stabilized.

A rasp from the next table roused him from a near-stupor.

No, I have to go home! one of the men shouted harshly. Stop! Don't pour more, I tell you! I can't drink anymore! The man rubbed the gray stubble on his chin and pushed his cup away.

Pleash, brother! It has—has been so—sho sho so long! The other fellow's articulation was terribly slurred.

I said no! I have to go home to feed my kids, don't I? The fucking bitch might work but she certainly leaves all the hard work to me. She almost never cooks and, if I don't, my kids will go hungry. *You* know nothing about it—and *she* doesn't care!

Know nothing? Know nothing? Lishen, I worked two damn shifts sh-sh-since yeshterday and I don't know if they'll pay me or not! Our fucking director ish an asshole! They sh-

sh-said revolutionary work, ish an honor! What kind of fuck-ing honor ish two shifts, back to back? Sh-sh-shit, I can't even talk straight. Come on, jussh one more cup!

At last they finished, kicked their chairs aside, grasped each other by the shoulders and reeled from the room, their voices receding into the distance: I'm alwayshh landed with two shifts . . . feed my kids . . . stupid fucking bitch . . .

He lit another cigarette, eyeing the packet on the table. Suddenly he recalled his brother-in-law's eyes, pitiful, adrift. *We all did our damn best.* His fingers tapped the packet rhythmically, like sullen raindrops.

The entrance door having been left ajar, a breeze swayed in, invigorating, indefinite. From outside he felt the scamper-ing awakenings of spring, faint rustlings, like grasshoppers on a late summer night—but also passersby, dragging their own shadows, their own burdens. He had been one of them but was one of them no longer.

Perhaps he never would be again.

Remembering the cat's satirical eyes, his frown deepened. Cats had nine lives. Or did they?

I have only one life, he said, too quietly for anyone to hear.

Then out of nowhere, he heard that girlish voice whisper-ing. It was an accident. It just—happened. He looked around swiftly, to see if anyone else had heard.

And all at once, he knew—he absolutely owned—what he

had done. And teetered, appalled, horrorstruck, on the edge of an abyss.

If only he could sit here and keep on drinking. If only he could find a place and go to sleep. Just for a while. Just for now. Just for the moment.

Maybe forever.

Yet as he raised his cup, his elbow bumped against the black bag beside him.

He was roused instantly. *I still have things to do! This day is only halfway finished. It isn't over yet. Hurry up! Leave!*

He reached into the bag and fingered the crisp money, the food ration stamps, thinking. *I could buy two sacks of flour, some rice too—if they have any rice in the grain shop.*

He stood up, a wry smile flickering over his face.

Noodles for dinner tonight.

BIOGRAPHICAL NOTE

Ruyan Meng was born and educated in China. She emigrated to the United States in the early 1990s. During the past decade she has immersed herself in Chinese history from the 1950s to the 1980s—the Stalinist-style oppression enforced by Mao Zedong. Her stories are inspired by true events in a "worker village" of the fifties—a residential compound directly copied from the Soviet Union. In her finely wrought tales, she has recreated this world: in microcosm, all human life is here. Ruyan Meng worked as an entrepreneur and real estate investor for twenty years, in Dallas, Texas. She now writes full-time and practices yoga and meditation.

9 781597 098762